ALL FOR THE LOVE OF

MARIE

ALL FOR THE LOVE OF
MARIE

ALWAYS KEEP A WARY EYE

JULIA FARGO

TATE PUBLISHING
AND ENTERPRISES, LLC

Published by Tate Publishing & Enterprises, LLC
127 E. Trade Center Terrace | Mustang, Oklahoma 73064 USA
1.888.361.9473 | www.tatepublishing.com

Tate Publishing is committed to excellence in the publishing industry. The company reflects the philosophy established by the founders, based on Psalm 68:11,
"The Lord gave the word and great was the company of those who published it."

Book design copyright © 2014 by Tate Publishing, LLC. All rights reserved.
Cover design by Ivan Charlem Igot
Interior design by Jake Muelle

Published in the United States of America

ISBN: 978-1-63367-372-4
Family & Relationships / Children with Special Needs
14.09.01

To my son, Joseph
You are a kind and caring brother
You never complain about the time and attention
Given to your sister
You are accepting of your sister and
love her unconditionally
You help your sister each day in many ways
You bring joy to your sister and her
eyes light up when she sees you
And when you talk to her
Thank you for being the sweetest boy and my precious gift

Love,
Mom

Contents

Where Her Battle in Life Became Known

To begin to describe what occurred at our daughter's battle for life and when we discovered she was not normal, or something was very wrong with our baby Marie, is going to be difficult. Before seven months old, we and even the doctors would describe her as a normal beautiful baby. She had olive skin and beautiful big brown eyes and curly brown hair. She laughed and smiled and was a happy bright baby. She came into the world after a long labor, but we never realized that something was wrong with her.

To begin Marie's story, on January 1, 2000, she was seven months old. Our world would be shattered. My husband Steve was ill with a stomach virus. I was sitting in our family room with Marie in my arms when she began throwing up and convulsing with her eyes rolled back in her head. As I held her, I realized I did not know what was happening to her. We quickly called 911, and I waited for what seemed like hours for the ambulance to come. Marie was convulsing in my arms as I carried her upstairs to wait for help. The EMTs arrived to help her, and all I could do was scream. "Help her before she dies!" I could not imagine losing her. She looked so pale and lifeless. The EMTs put an oxygen mask on her and informed me that she was having a seizure. I then carried her in my arms out to the ambulance and held her tight, trying to get myself together and not think of anything but to help her.

My husband had called her grandparents and immediately rushed to a hospital. I told the EMTs that I wanted Marie to go to the hospital I had always gone to but they told me, "No, she is going to the children's hospital." I did not even know there was a children's hospital in the area. As Marie was rushed to the hospital, I don't really remember what was happening and was still holding on to her for what dear little life she had. We got to the hospital and she was rushed into a room where every tube a monitor could have was hooked up to her. The doctors had ordered the nurses to give her great amounts of antiseizure medication. The seizures continued for hours in the emergency room as we stood by and watched her slip more and more away from life. The doctors then said to admit her and move her up to a room. As we arrived, a team of doctors and nurses filled the room. Marie's grandparents were also in the room, but her father could not come to the hospital as he was still not feeling well. I remember my father saying when we thought Marie had finally stopped seizing, "Marie is still seizing or she is going into distress again!" The doctor looked at her again and said, "Yes, she is." I remember the intern asking how much more he should give her as he already had given her the maximum amount. The doctor said that it was too much and not to give her any more. She should be okay. Marie did finally stop seizing.

I remember walking into the room as the nurse recognized me, or I remembered her as we had bought her house two years ago. This nurse had comforted me by telling me that I have the best doctor and how lucky we were to have him because he is the teaching doctor at this hospital.

The day went on and Marie just slept. The doctors just couldn't believe how much medication it took to get her to stop having the convulsive seizures. She was okay the next day and slept.

Throughout the whole day, Marie's father was still not able to visit her as he was so sick, and they did not want him around Marie with his germs. I told the doctor that they were pumping too much medication into her still. The doctor had explained to me that they weren't, and they are watching her carefully. After, not convinced of his answer, I began to get upset and walked off leaving my parents and my husband's parents in the room. I went to cool off and my mother had to come downstairs to find me and to explain that the doctor was sorry he didn't realize they were still medicating her so drastically. I went back upstairs to Marie's room still upset but thought I better shut up and listen. He did tell me the meds would be dropped down to see if she comes to. I recall yelling at him, "I am not sure who this baby is. I don't even see the baby I brought in!" After things calmed down, I went and sat and continued staring at Marie as that's all I seemed to be able to do.

I could not eat or sleep; I just wanted my beautiful Baby Marie back. After three days, her dad was finally allowed to see her as he was so upset at home not to be with her.

After five days in the hospital, the doctors had determined Marie had the seizure possibly due to a fever or an illness.

We left the hospital with the medication for seizures, just as a precaution, to be sure she would be okay and not to have anymore seizures.

We were only home a day or two when Marie began seizing again and convulsing. As I looked at her, she was covered head to toe with a severe rash and was burning up. Steve quickly called 911 again. I held her tight and freaked out again. We were then rushed to the hospital by ambulance and Marie was put at the same area in the emergency room. All the doctors and nurses began administering the same antiseizure drugs and the same great amounts. She still convulsed and they rushed her up to intensive care. Marie did, after maybe three or four hours of seizing, stop convulsing. She slept again like a baby for hours. The nurses were wonderful to her and me, as I can remember one saying, "Go down the hall and get some sleep," and she would call me when Marie wakes up. I did manage to pull myself away from her about 12:00 a.m. Well, the nurse called me at 5:30 a.m. to tell me Marie was awake. The nurse said Marie had been up most of the night screaming a playful scream all night. The nurse explained to me that they had just passed her around to all nurses as each one took turns carrying Marie, and held her through the night, because she would not sleep. We later discovered this was a reaction to the medication she was given; the neurons in her brain kept firing and it made her vocal and hyper.

Eventually, Marie would stop and go to sleep; "eventually" meaning eight to ten hours sometimes.

We were then sent to a regular floor in the children's hospital. They were able to let us go home after getting Marie's seizures under control with the new medication.

This pattern of living—Marie being rushed to the hospital every two to four weeks, depending on how long the medications would not reject her system—became almost a habit. I am, sort of, skipping a lot of the same familiar details as we would run back and forth to the hospital. Marie became a regular and a familiar patient to the ambulance EMTs and the doctors in the hospital. I can recall one doctor saying, "It's Marie again, get all the meds ready." God only knows how long she will keep up as we entered the emergency room once again. She was still just a tiny baby and each time we had to go to the hospital, my adrenalin would pump and I would go through the same familiar emotions and my world would be spinning so fast—if only I could stop it. I can remember each time so vividly. I can also remember begging her to please stop! Please don't go so long with your seizures as the last time! But she always would keep seizing.

Life Keeps Throwing Us a Curveball

Marie was taking her new seizure medication and things seemed okay. That is, until about two weeks after getting out of the hospital, Marie began seizing again. We called 911 and the ambulance had rushed her to the hospital. As we came in, the doctors realized who it was and I remember all of them, all the nurses and doctors saying, "Oh no! It's Marie again!" They began pumping the medication into her and trying to get her to stop seizing. After several hours, Marie stopped seizing and was sent up to intensive care. Since the nurses upstairs recognized her, they began to get ready for her. She was sleeping for awhile but woke up screaming, and they assured me it was okay and to go down the hall to sleep in the parent's overnight sleeping room as they had other times. I woke up as they called me and said she was sleeping after staying up all night screaming her head off.

We went down to a floor she had been on before and the nurses recognized her there, too. The nurses were actually fighting over who would take care of Marie, because she was such a great baby and a joy. I have to say so being her proud mother. We stayed for a few days and the doctors put her on another new medication. We then went home trying the meds and Marie doing her usual baby stuff.

Then, about two weeks went by and Marie began seizing again. Well, we had figured out the drill by now and called 911 and they rushed her to the children's hospital. She was placed in the same room and they worked on her and she finally stopped seizing. The same nurses were there to greet her and they took such great care of her. Once more, we went down to the floor and we met the same doctors and nurses. She would get the best treatment, as she was always treated with such great compassionate care. I can recall my mother-in-law walking Marie up and around the hallways for hours it seems to get her to stop yelling and to go to sleep. My mother-in-law was so tired but she just wouldn't stop pushing Marie in the wagon trying to get her to calm down to sleep. Thank goodness for my mother-in-law, as Marie wore out everyone, I would try to hold her to calm her down after the medications wore off. We then went home with another new medication to give her.

Marie was nine months old by now and the doctors were no longer thinking this was an illness which causes Marie to seize, but rather a condition she has. We were told she may outgrow this condition, but she may also not. We were absorbed in Marie's world as we tried to continue on with our lives, but it became difficult. I went back to work and so did my husband. We would miss days from work when she would end up in the hospital.

Marie went back to her routine, which was staying at her grandma's during my work hours—I worked for the school system to tutor kids with special needs. People will often ask me if that's how I came to be working with kids with special needs because of Marie. My response was no, because I was pregnant with her when I began working with the kids at school. I was pregnant prior to working with special needs kids and wanted a job that wasn't too stressful. I had lost my first child, so I didn't tell anyone I was pregnant with Marie until after three months. I had applied for a job that had pretty much violent kids and knew if I was going to keep this baby, I better not take the job due to the fact I was so afraid of losing my second pregnancy. Not sure why I mention this, but I suppose to let you know I made a great effort to take care of this baby after losing my first.

Anyway, as life went on, we had to make new arrangements for Marie to have someone watch her at our home. Marie was getting into a sleep pattern of staying up at night, and we didn't want to disturb her when she would finally go to sleep. She sometimes, I can recall, fell asleep at midnight or one in the morning and just moved every part of her body. She didn't seem to be uncomfortable but you couldn't sleep until she was sleeping, after wearing herself out. When I would ask the doctors why she does this, I can remember one smiling and saying, as if it's cute, "We don't know."

I had asked my older sister, Mary, to watch her as she said she would. My sister knew her so well and I could only leave her with family. My sister did take her everywhere she went and adored her. Marie enjoyed being with her aunt Mary and lit up when Mary would call her by the nickname of Boo Boo. Mary did spoil Marie, and Marie enjoyed her naps with Mary everyday on my bed. It became a problem after a while as Marie no longer wanted to sleep in her crib and just wanted to stay in our bed as she napped with her aunt each day. I eventually had to let Marie fuss for a while to get her back to her crib. Believe me, I don't like a baby to cry, so I did this for weeks before I could actually leave her in her crib. When I say I couldn't stand it, I mean minutes not hours, but we did it as my husband and I took turns consoling Marie to get her to sleep. I also had to break the habit with Aunt Mary, as nap time in my bed needed to stop for Marie and Aunt Mary.

Life was going okay. Marie still had seizures but mostly at night. We did have Valium at home to give Marie, but most of the time, that didn't stop the seizures.

Where Do We Go from Here?

We have been back and forth to the children's hospital for the past year. We already had an organization called Birth to Three come to our home to help us get Marie mobile. I can recall when the Birth to Three teachers had come in, I was in complete denial. I refused to believe my daughter would need a walker or a stander to use for everyday activities. The physical therapist gave us all sorts of exercises to get Marie to roll over and crawl. Marie just laid there as much as we wanted her to move and you begged her to move, it just couldn't happen. I told the Birth to Three teacher, each time she worked with Marie, that it's just not coming along. The teacher and speech and physical therapist would try new strategies. Marie once grabbed her bottle from the teacher and we were grateful for her acting that way as she did have some responses. We would sit Marie up and she would roll right over. Eventually, she did learn to sit up and put her hands down to support herself, although she flipped one hand always instead of hands down—she would have one up and one down when sitting.

At times, we could not get Marie to respond. It was as if we weren't even there. We weren't sure if she was looking at us because it's either she was having a seizure or in her own world. She would smile and laugh if you jumped her on the bed or tickled her. She had the biggest smile and was the happiest baby. Birth to Three, I can remember, tried faking a scolding or just trying to see if she would react to anger and she wouldn't.

We were still going to the hospital but not as often. We went about once a month instead of every two weeks. Marie was two years old and the hospital was running out of medications to treat Marie's seizures; she had been put on so many. I asked one of the neurologists who knew Marie. "What do we do now? Should we be looking into another hospital to treat her?" His answer was, "Yes, we really are running out of options to treat Marie." The doctor had told us of another children's hospital in the state and of another neurologist. We then made an appointment with the neurologist who was among the best in the state.

Marie was now two years old by now and we were still desperate to cure our daughter. We began seeing the new neurologist. The new neurologist was great and knew everything there was to know about seizures. We made appointments every two to three months as Marie was going through medications there, too. We were told to do a sleep study which required around twenty to forty electrodes to be placed in her scalp using a special glue to keep the electrodes in her head. It was the most difficult procedure Marie had to endure. She cried and screamed as each probe was put in.

We could just try to console her and hope each one was the last to be placed. My husband and I were practically in tears to watch this baby have to go through this procedure. Marie had to do the sleep study and an electroencephalogram (EEG). The EEG was to tell us where the seizures were coming from in her brain. It showed us the spikes that would record the brain waves and the activated parts of the brain that showed seizure activity. Marie had this turban on her head because her head was wrapped in gauze to keep the electrodes in place for the test.

We were all set for the overnight study and trying to settle Marie in. We were told the hospital didn't have Marie's diaper size. We didn't have any with us, so my husband had to go out at eleven at night and find diapers. He did find the diapers. My husband was staying at a hotel; I was staying with my mother-in-law at the hospital to be with Marie. Marie was sleeping and then I noticed her having a seizure. I yelled for the nurse to come and take a look at her. The nurse came in and discovered she was having a grand mal seizure and also noticed Marie was having difficulty breathing. The nurse quickly grabbed the oxygen mask and put it on Marie. She soon noticed when she was trying to give Marie meds to stop the seizures that the oxygen wasn't hooked up to the wall correctly. I then grabbed the oxygen mask and put it over her mouth and held it there to get her air. The nurse then called the intern and asked for help. The intern, I'll never forget her for the rest of my life, was not concerned and acted as if she couldn't be bothered. She just walked in, gave an order and walked out, and then went to the nurses' station to do some paperwork. She just didn't give a damn.

The nurse was still trying to get Marie to stop seizing; maybe it was fifteen minutes into this episode, but it seemed like hours. I was getting hysterical as was my mother-in-law. We just kept asking for help and the nurse was trying so hard to do everything she could. She then said she was going to call Marie's neurologist who I knew was leaving on an overseas trip that night. The neurologist could not come in but sent the fellow who knew Marie. Before he could get there, things were getting worse. I, by the way, was six months pregnant and just worried about Marie but trying not to get too stressed with the baby I was carrying. All of a sudden, a team of about six or seven doctors went flying into Marie's room. The doctors threw us out of the room and we were standing out in the hallway as I saw all the doors being closed on the floor and heard over the loud speaker: "Code Blue" and the floor number we were on being called. I remember saying to my mother-in-law, "Is that for Marie?" My mother-in-law was so shaken up and didn't want to upset me so she said she didn't know. I thought things were getting out of control and I had better call Steve at the hotel. My mother-in-law said she would call Steve and let him know Marie was having trouble with seizures. Marie was still being worked on in the room as they couldn't find a vein to get the medication in to stop the seizures. My husband arrived and then immediately rushed in. After, a security guard now was being called. When I asked why security was called, I was told in case my husband got any more out of control because he was yelling at them to do something for Marie. The doctors then came out and told us they would have to move her up to Intensive Care to work on her.

We then were escorted up to Intensive Care and told to stay in the waiting room and they would keep us informed of what was happening.

I remember asking the head doctor if Marie was going to die. All she could tell me was that they were doing their best to save her. The "fellow" finally arrived upstairs and I just let him have it. I screamed at him telling him that if Marie dies, I would sue the hell out of this hospital. Not that I ever would because at this point I needed them more than they needed me. I had screamed at him about the intern that would not help care for Marie after the nurse repeatedly tried to get her to help. I had told him they should have been ready for this and they said they were. The staff should have been ready to expect this from Marie as they knew her seizures were so intense and very difficult to get her out of them. The hospital was informed from her previous experiences with seizures about how awful they could become. The "fellow" just felt sorry for us and he genuinely cared about Marie but was lost on how to help. The doctor who worked on Marie finally came out to us at about 1:00 a.m. and said they finally stopped the seizures and Marie was stable. The doctor said we could go see her and warned us that she had a lot of tubes connected to her. She needed to be put on a breathing machine; I think it is called a ventilator. She also had medication being pumped into her. She had a tube in her stomach area since that was the only place they could get an IV in. We went in and I could remember how awful she looked. This little baby girl all hooked up to tubes and machines. How ugly looking. All I could think of and say to her was how sorry I was for bringing her here and feeling like I was the one who did this to her. The three of us—my husband, my mother-in-law, and me—just cried when we saw her. And I couldn't hold her; all I could do was stare in amazement and wonder what was going to happen to her. We just wanted her to live and be back with us no matter how she would be.

We were told to give her time and let her sleep. It was about 5:00 a.m. when we went back to our room. Steve went back to the hotel to get some rest. I told him I would call if and when Marie woke up. Marie did wake up in a few hours. I can remember them bringing her back down to the floor where she originally began the testing. I was so happy to see her. I just wanted to hold her and did because all the tubes were out. We even laughed at ourselves after about how crazy we were and how we behaved, especially me, since I was so tough on the doctors. We were able to leave the hospital the next day and did do the EEG test the night before. I would say we just went through hell instead of poor little Marie. She came back to herself as time went on.

I had called my family while all this was going on, and my parents were eager to know what was happening. My sister, who took care of Marie, noticed—more than us—that Marie was just not the same after that event. She still thinks that Marie suffered some brain damage and never came back to her full base line.

Life went on and we were happy to be home after the exhausting trip from the hospital. We received the test results, which to top it off, were not helpful as the doctor said Marie's seizures were all over her brain, and they couldn't pinpoint where the seizures were coming from. They couldn't say because they were all over the right side and left side of the brain.

Steve and I went back to work again and tried to live our life as normally as we could. Marie continues to have her seizures, but we can use the Valium and we can control the seizures better now.

Is There a Cure?

After three months went by, we began to seek out and find exactly what Marie's diagnosis was. We only knew that we have a little girl with a seizure disorder and she can't talk or walk. Marie was two years old and we still had no diagnosis or prognosis for her future. I began calling her pediatrician's office and asking for a referral to go to a doctor outside the state to see if we could get another opinion. The doctor from the pediatrician's office told me, "Mrs. Fargo, I don't know what you are looking for and why you don't stop trying to find answers? Your daughter is retarded or as they say now a days, developmentally delayed and that is all there is." I recall saying to him, "What do you mean retarded? How did she get this way?" I told him there was no apparent reason when she was born and no one has said that to me. He said, "Well, I'm telling you now!" I don't remember saying anymore to him, but I was shocked at his remarks to me. After hanging up, I thought, *The hell with him. I will do this on my own.*

We then went to a hospital in Boston to meet with a doctor who was just coming on staff at one of the children's hospitals. She told us we could run tests like another EEG to find the source of the seizures and run more blood work. We did bring the entire test we had done, but she really could not give us any answers at that time either.

We then decided to go back to the second children's hospital as we looked into ways to help find a cure for Marie's condition. We were given a name of a neurosurgeon. After seeing the neurosurgeon, he suggested taking out a part of Marie's brain to stop the seizures.

The surgery sounded like it could help her. We were ecstatic to finally have a solution to her problem. The neurosurgeon explained to us there would be a lot of tests that she would have to undergo and the risks involved in the surgery. After the tests results were in, the doctors said that they would all meet to determine if Marie would be a good candidate for the brain surgery. If not, the brain surgery would not be performed.

It was now December of 2001 and we were told we could begin the testing for Marie's brain surgery. If we wanted to go through with it, we were to begin testing right away. So we went to the hospital and did, if I can remember correctly, this one test. Marie had to be put to sleep for the test; I believe it was the MRI. They did not want Marie to move at all during the test. As Steve was carrying her around the hospital from room to room, he began having chest pains. He told me in passing before this, but through all the craziness of our lives, I told him, "Your fine, you'll be all right." This time as we were going in the room for the test, Steve just didn't seem right. He finally said, "I don't feel good." And he went completely pale and looked weak. The nurse said to him, "Would you like me to carry Marie? You don't look very well, Mr. Fargo." I was eight months pregnant, and the nurse must have looked at me like you can't carry her either lady. Steve did hand Marie over to the nurse and she took her to the test. Steve went to sit down and then said he was feeling better and he was all right now. Me being the sensitive and caring wife, I just put it aside and wanted to get finished with the test. When Marie finished the MRI and they had the information they needed, we left to go home.

We had a forty-five minute ride home. Steve was driving and he said again he wasn't feeling so well. I, of course, the intelligent women I am said, "What are you talking about chest pains? Do you think you're having a heart attack?" Steve didn't know what he was having but I thought well enough is enough with my stupidity and lack of sensitivity; I will call his doctor now on the cell phone. So I did! The doctor was about as sensitive as I was. He said as I explained Steve's symptoms, "Is he having a heart attack?" I said, "I don't know. I'm not a doctor. How should I know?" My sarcasm was certainly not helping the situation. The doctor then told me I should take him to the emergency room if he is having a heart attack. I then said something to the effect I wasn't sure what he was having. It was more like a conversation of who's on first and getting nowhere. Steve refused to go to the doctor but promised in the morning he would go. It was December 5, 2000, and Steve went to the hospital. When he got there, they took him immediately and told him he was having a mild heart attack. The doctors said to me when I went to see him a couple of hours later that he was lucky he made it. I felt more guilt as I saw him lying there and hooked up to a heart monitor. The doctor then said he had to undergo an operation called angioplasty in order to insert a stent. Steve was only thirty-four years old and he already had heart problems. Heart conditions are in his family on both sides so the chance of him getting this condition was very high. Steve had the surgery the next day and he was fine.

Marie was going with my family to a Christmas party. My father brought all the grandchildren to this party every year. I was trying to go visit Steve in the hospital and my sister was coming over with her six-month-old and Marie, now being two, to take them to the party. I was a wreck but knew she had to go and my sister could handle taking the two little ones. I was on the phone and Steve was trying to call me, (we had caller ID) and I didn't pick up his call as I was talking to my sister to make arrangements for Marie, car seats, sippy cups, diapers, and so on. I was so nervous. Anyway, when I called Steve back, and still to this day, he never will let me live it down about how I didn't pick up the phone while he was so called "dying" in the hospital from his heart condition. I now and then said to him, "You were fine. You had had the operation and you were in a hospital. If anything was going to happen to you, you were in the right place, so relax!" After a couple of days, Steve came home and was recovering. I thought I had to do my penance and wait on him hand and foot while he recovered. Boy did I pay! Just kidding, he was doing well. So we move on to another chapter in our lives.

Steve went back to work after a couple of weeks. I did the same and waited for our new arrival to come. It became tougher for me to get around, and I became more tired with my pregnancy. My obstetrician wanted me to take it easy and give up my job. I couldn't give up my job. I needed to work financially; hospital bills were adding up. Between Steve and Marie, the bills were starting to mount up as we both missed days from work. Neither Steve nor I got paid for any time we missed. So we continued to work, and as I said, life went on. We still had more testing to do for

Marie's upcoming surgery which was scheduled for May of 2001.

It was September 8, 2001, when Marie had a cold and a fever. She was having a seizure and then another and another. We couldn't get her seizures under control again so we had to call 911. The hospital was packed, and the EMTs rushed Marie into the emergency room and they gave her a room right away. Marie's seizure had kept coming and the medication was not working until finally, after around a half an hour, her seizures stopped. The doctors said she needed to stay overnight because of her having a high fever and to be watched for more seizures. The doctor had told us there were no beds available at this hospital, but they could fly Marie by Life Star helicopter to another children's hospital in the state. I was not going to be able to go in with her because the doctors said this is just not something they allow for parents to go in the helicopter with the patient. I was not happy but had to go with their rules. I thought we will race down to the hospital and just have to get there shortly after Marie lands there. I have never left her alone in any place let alone a hospital. I have such a trust issue or not so much trust but know mistakes can happen, and I fear the hospital staff might make a mistake since they are so busy. After making all of the arrangements to have Marie flown down to the other children's hospital in the state, we receive a call from the intensive care unit of the hospital Marie was still in and waiting for Marie to be transported by air. Well, the nurse on the intensive care unit said, "You didn't tell us it was for Marie Fargo. We will always find a bed or make room for her." I was so relived and glad we did not have to go to the other children's hospital. We were then taken up to the floor of intensive care and the nurses were all happy to see Marie. The doctor said, "It is a good thing Marie is so popular in this hospital because the nurses aren't usually able to make accommodations. Marie must be loved here." The nurses did tell me after that from now on don't ever hesitate to tell the emergency room that ICU would always take Marie. Make sure the next time you tell them to call ICU to make room for Marie. The nurses were always so unbelievably kind and cared so much for Marie.

Marie did stay overnight and we went to a regular floor and she was released in a couple of days. Her seizures had stopped and her cold was much better. This was just another incident with Marie that I never think could get out of control, and we were not sure where Marie was going with the seizure episodes.

Life Starts to Get Brighter

Marie was doing better and her seizures have calmed down for the time being. It was Super Bowl, Sunday, January 28, 2001; I put Marie in her crib for a nap. I wasn't feeling so great and Steve was going to a friend's house to watch the Super Bowl. I told him I was fine and to go ahead and watch the game. Well, he was gone about an hour and a half, and then I called him at his friend's house and said, "My water just broke, can you come home?" He responded, "Now?" I said to him, "No, not now! Why don't you stay and watch the game and I'll go tomorrow to have this baby!" I think he was really in shock and didn't think I was going to have this baby today. Steve then called his parents to come and take care of Marie and they were going to keep her at their house. On our way to the hospital, my dear, sweet, caring husband had the audacity to ask if we could stop along the way at his friend's house to grab a beer for the road. I, like an idiot, let him as my water leaked all over his cherished car. When we went by his friend's house, they all ran out handing him a beer and wishing us luck as my husband left beeping the horn, and my contractions are coming faster and faster.

We got to the hospital and our baby was born, right after the Super Bowl was over. Thank goodness. The baby was a healthy eight-pound baby boy. We named him Joseph Samuel. Joseph was black and blue when he came out. As

I was told, he came out so fast; he must have gotten black and blue coming through the birth canal. He had the face only a mother could love as he was so bruised. Steve always said to me, "What a horrible thing to say about our son being so homely." We loved him and were just so happy and relieved he was healthy unlike his sister. We were so afraid that he may turn out the same way Marie did. We hadn't planned on having another child, not right away anyway, not until we knew what was wrong with Marie.

Both sets of grandparents came in at one in the morning to see Joseph, as they were so excited to see him. The next day, when my mother-in-law came to see Joseph, I can remember asking her how Marie was doing and if she enjoys having a new brother? She told me, "Marie was Lucka Ducking all day." At the time, this was one of Marie's favorite things to say, as she did have just a couple of words in her vocabulary. After a couple of days, we then took Joseph home to meet his sister.

Marie didn't seem too impressed with her new brother but seemed to tolerate him. Marie was only twenty-one months older than Joseph. Life was chaotic with having really two babies in the house now. We also had two cats and one dog, a Dalmatian, Max.

Everyone seemed to be getting adjusted to our life and things seemed to be going smooth. Marie still had her seizures and we watched her all night on a baby video camera and Joe on a baby monitor too.

Steve's friends Chip and Peter and the rest of his friends had decided they were going to have a benefit for Marie or in her honor. It was March 10, 2001. So they were to have the benefit for Marie and for us to cover some medical expenses we had of co-pays and equipment not covered by insurance and time we lost from not being able to work. So the benefit went on and it seems the whole town of Newington, CT., where we live, came. It was so wonderful to have all our friends and family come to the benefit. The community really reached out in so many ways and donated so much from food to raffle prizes, to a friend being a DJ for the evening. We were so grateful and can still never repay everyone for their kindness, especially Chip and Peter, for all they did. I can recall going in with Steve and the two babies, Marie and Joseph, and being just overwhelmed with the number of people there. It was a packed hall to say the least. They said that the fire marshal, if he had known, would have to clear the building as there were so many people in the hall. Marie took everything in stride as everyone was snapping her picture and it was so loud. As the night went on, Marie did get tired and we had to bring her home. Her baby brother just slept through the whole thing since he was only two months old.

We were as grateful, as I said, to Chip and Peter as we would not have been able to pay our bills had it not been for them giving us the benefit in Marie's honor. We did pay the hospital bills and purchased some equipment that we needed for Marie. We had to get a fax machine and we were able to now with the benefit money. We had to fax forms back and forth to doctors and hospitals, signing release forms and so forth. We were also able to buy Marie a new car seat as she was getting bigger.

I can also remember telling Chip and Pete to take some money as they were giving it to us from the benefit, but they refused to take a dime. As times were so hard back then, I can remember being so optimistic after they did the benefit. I just was always worried about the bills as they piled up and not ever knowing how we were going to ever pay for them. I can remember thinking things work out somehow, they always do for us.

What a relief it was for us to know we could move on with Marie's surgery and focus on her and Joe again 100 percent.

We were going to make it, so we did. We again began to focus on more tests for Marie and we trucked back and forth to the children's hospital for more tests.

Just One More Test to Go!

There was one more test to do as we got ready for Marie's brain surgery in April of 2001. The one test we hated more than Marie—it was the EEG. We had to do another overnight sleep study to be sure of the location of the seizures. The doctors had figured out by then where the seizures were coming from but had to be sure. We got Marie to the hospital and she started to get the electrodes put in her head. Mind you, these are put in with like a super glue gun to keep every electrode in place. Marie is again screaming and crying due to the pain and touching her head. She became so intolerant of people touching her head as time went on in her life due to the seizures and probably having her head touched so much. She had to take breaks. The technician doing the procedure knew her by then and was so kind to her let her stop to get a rest from the process. We finally got them all in. I stated before there are twenty to thirty, I believe, that have to go into her head to get a reading. Marie was then taken to the room where they did the study and settled in. My husband and I were uptight from the last time we did the EEG, which was disastrous to say the least.

We were watching TV and Marie was moving quite a bit and her little "turban" was coming apart. We tried to fix it but were not successful and decided we should probably call the nurse. The nurse came in and she was in a hurry and busy and said that she would fix the wrap on Marie's head so the electrodes wouldn't come out. Steve told the nurse, "Be careful don't cut the electrodes," as she was about to cut a piece of the gauze to fix the wrapping. I told Steve, "She knows what she's doing, she won't cut them." Well, she took the scissors and cut all the wires or electrodes as they are called, right off. We all thought we were going to have a heart attack right then and there. Marie wasn't bothered by it; they were cut at the ends of the wires. The nurse was in such shock; all she could say was, "I'm sorry. I can't believe I did that." It meant Marie would have to start all over again and it was eleven at night, not that any time was good. The nurse then called the fellow who was the neurologist we knew, and was Marie's doctor when the neurologist wasn't there. The fellow, I forgot his name, said, "I can't believe this. What's with you guys? We can't seem to get it right down here with you." The fellow meant that the last time we were in this hospital, they screwed up with the code blue incident. He asked us what do we want to do, either start again and put the electrodes back in her or go home and start again another time. Meanwhile, Marie is sound asleep throughout this whole crisis. The technician came in and said he could have done it very carefully and placed the electrodes in so Marie wouldn't feel it. We thought about it and decided we were already there and if we could have it done so she would not feel it then we'll do it again. So we woke her up and carried her to the room down the hall where they put the electrodes in.

Marie is screaming and now fully awakened as the electrodes are being put on her again. It took about an hour, maybe quicker, but seems like twenty hours to get them all back in her head.

We got her back in her bed after holding her and consoling her, she fell asleep and the test went on. The doctors got the information they needed and we headed for home the next day. Taking the electrodes out is almost as painful but not quite as bad as putting them in. They don't have to put pressure on her head to get them off. The glue is fun trying to get washed out of her hair. It usually took a couple of washings and to get the entire pink marker out was a challenge too. I swore to Marie I would never make her go through that test again, and I don't think we ever did, not the overnight glue gun EEG. The regular EEG is not so bad. She doesn't like it; it was more irritating than painful.

We then were ready to proceed with the surgery and had the entire test out of the way. When we got home, we got a call from a local TV station anchorwoman who said she wanted to do a story on Marie. The story they wanted to run was about children having this brain surgery at the children's hospital. The doctor had already asked us if we would mind if we went public with Marie's upcoming brain surgery. We told the doctor we didn't mind, seeing it would inform other patients and that we would be helping others who are not aware of this surgical procedure as a possible cure for them. The anchorwoman was due to come over the following morning to interview us.

The interview was set for 10:00 a.m. The house was a mess and we had to go like crazy cleaning late into the night. We went to bed and when we woke up, Marie was having one of her crying days. We did everything to try to calm her down. We would change her, feed her, rock her, and take turns between my husband and myself. Sometimes, Joseph would start crying the minute he saw or heard her cry. We would have to stop both of them, or I would start panicking and tell my husband to take her or Joseph out to the other room. I hated to hear a baby or children cry especially our own, so it became a real circus when this trauma would start. Marie's crying spells could go on for hours for no reason and as I said, we would go crazy, to say the least, during those times. If someone came to our home, they would think we were all nuts! Getting back to the news anchorwoman who was supposedly coming, well, she had called to cancel the interview because another story had come up. I guess our story wasn't so important and we were dropped. I tried to call the next day to find out when she was coming out to do Marie's story, but I guess she wasn't interested in us anymore. I never received an answer.

Well, we finally found out from the doctors why Marie had been crying for months. It turned out it was the antiseizure medications making her depressed since some seizure meds are antidepressants and can have the reverse effect on some people. We had just figured it was Marie and we had to deal with it. The doctor changed medications again and soon the crying stopped as we weaned her off of the old one. It did happen again later on with another medication, but we were smart enough by then to call the doctor to get her on something else. Marie always had some sort of side effects to medications.

Marie went back to her routine as I did. I enjoyed staying at home with both my kids while I could be with them.

Marie's Brain Surgery

We had everything packed and ready to go to the hospital; it was May 6, 2002. The hospital admitted Marie quickly and set her up in a room. The next day, Marie would have a part of her skull removed to insert a grid in her brain to track the seizures or brain waves. We knew beforehand this was going to be a two-part surgery. The first part was taking a four-inch part of the skull off and placing the grid in her brain for tracking. She was put in intensive care and watched on monitors. I can remember going in to see her. She was just lying there; her head was making all kinds of movements. The nurse said she didn't know why Marie was moving her head so much. They had to watch her because they were gradually taking off her seizure meds to get better results. We had to start weaning her off the meds at home in order not to send her system into shock from withdrawal. Another doctor approached me and said they were doing another whole different set of procedures. I didn't understand the plan, and I was shocked and demanded to see the neurosurgeon. The neurosurgeon came in and informed me what the other doctor was saying was not true and that he was in charge; Marie was his only patient for the surgery and the surgery procedure was to go as planned. I was relieved. All I could think of was here we go again with this hospital which had screwed up before.

You may wonder why we agreed to this surgery and the simple answer was we were running out of options and so desperate to fix Marie.

After being in intensive care for two days, she was then moved to another floor to observe more of her brain activity. There was a whole team of doctors and specialists who came into Marie's room and hooked her up to machines. The doctors explained to us they wanted to see if Marie would react when stimulating a part of the brain and see if different body parts would move. So they did the test and hooked up the electrodes to her brain. She did move the body parts as she was programmed to. They finished the test and left. About two hours later, a team of doctors came in. One of them I recognized as she had filled in for Marie's neurologist in the past while he was away. This female neurologist came right over to us and said, "We were unable to locate the damaged part of Marie's brain and therefore we will not be doing the rest of the surgery. We will not take out any part of her brain. We just don't know where or what part to remove." She was so nonchalant about her news that my husband and I were so shocked. Steve said, "You have got to be kidding me? Are you serious? We did all this for nothing?" The doctor said, "I don't see the problem." Then my husband left the room to calm down and get his frustration out. The doctor turned to me and said, "What is the problem? I don't understand why you are both so upset." I stood in disbelief. I turned and said, "You don't get it. We just had our daughter's head cracked open and did all this for nothing. She gains nothing from all this stress and pain we had to make her endure once again." The doctor still looked at me like sorry, life's tough, get over it and left the room.

I just left and went downstairs to the lobby outside to get some air. I called my family on my cell phone to let them know the disappointing news. I cried for Marie again and felt so guilty for putting her through all of this stress and discomfort again. It was a day later and they put the part of her skull back in her head and sewed her up and let her recover. It was so hard to see her with her bald head and about 20 staples running across her head. As I held her after the surgery, she just looked at me as if to say "It's okay mommy. I'm all right." Marie was such a good little girl; she was the strongest of all of us and made us get through everything. She was so tolerant and everyone always commented on what a good girl she was. She always came through in the end of all her turmoil, back to her happy little self.

We stayed in the hospital for another week waiting for Marie to recuperate from the surgery. Her grandmother and grandfather came in to see her and they brought Joseph with them as they had been taking care of him while we were at the hospital. Joe was a quiet little baby and was sixteen months old by now. Steve and I missed him so much; we were both very glad to see him. We spent as much time as we could during their visit. It was so difficult to say good-bye to Joseph when it was time for them to leave because we had to stay at the hospital with Marie. We were so torn; we wanted to be with Joseph but knew we had to be with Marie through the surgery.

Marie just slept and slept as we waited each day for her to wake up after the surgery. She finally started coming around. She was looking alert and more like herself. We then were told we could leave in a day or two. Marie was being gradually put back on her normal seizure meds and tolerating food again. We left the hospital on May 16 and went home.

We started settling back into our life again and Joseph was back home with us. Marie did sleep most of the days, just waking up to eat a little. Marie was turning three years old on May 21, 2002.

We had a very small family party as everyone wanted to see Marie after the surgery. She was tired and could only stay up and sit in her high chair for a little while. We had pictures of her with her birthday cake, and she looked so much bigger and growing so tall. I still felt the guilt for all she went through. Marie, at her birthday, again looked at me as if to say it's okay mommy, I'm all right.

We continued on with Marie still recovering at a good pace. We had to bring her back the following week for a follow-up visit to the hospital. We went and had the staples removed as Marie cried as the nurse removed them. We also spoke to the neurosurgeon and expressed our disappointment in the results of the surgery for Marie. We thought it was going to be the break we were hoping for. The doctor said the information that was previously gathered and all the tests had really been not consistent with what was now happening in Marie's brain. In other words, the time lapse between the times Marie went into surgery and the tests were old and they didn't match what her brain had been showing at the time of the surgery. He explained that there was no way of knowing that Marie's seizure activity had changed and they couldn't locate the damaged part of the brain to be removed. We certainly, as we told the doctors, didn't want them just to remove a piece of her brain for no apparent reason, but we had thought they had found the information beforehand. Anyway, to us, there was no sense in dwelling on this tragedy but to move forward again for the sake of Marie.

Beginning of School

Birth to Three had been involved in all of Marie's therapeutic and teaching skills from nine months to three years of age. They had taught us so much on how to adapt and teach Marie to function in life as best she could. They had set up the state programs and other resources we would need for Marie over the years. We had to meet with her new school as she was going to a public school in our town and to begin preschool at three years old. We met with the Birth to Three staff that worked with Marie and also met with her new school staff to get her prepared for preschool in the fall. There must have been twenty people sitting at the table that would care for Marie in the upcoming school year. There was an occupational therapist, a speech therapist, a physical therapist, nurses, tutors, a special education supervisor, and teachers, and then there were the five or six staff members from Birth to Three. We had given Marie's history and tried to describe her condition as best we could. Marie was either in my husband's arms or mine during this whole, maybe two hours, meeting with the school staff and Birth to Three. They were all very kind and seemed very concerned for Marie's well-being.

After the meeting with the school staff, we had everything in place. Marie was going to school in the fall of 2002.

The summer had gone well. Marie did go to the town's summer program for two hours three days a week as a trial period for the fall preschool program. Things were going well and Marie enjoyed the summer school as they were so sweet to her. Everyone loved her; she was so happy and just glad to be there. (She was adorable as everyone always told me, even if I do have to brag myself.) After her surgery, she was still so bald and needed to wear a hat at all times for fear the sun would burn her head. All summer, we went to the cottage that my parents owned a lot. Marie loved the beach and going in the water. My family and Steve's family always came down to the cottage on weekends.

My dad had passed away the previous year in October of 2001. He really enjoyed Marie and loved holding her. Although he was getting frail toward the end of his life, he always wanted to hold her. He loved coming down in the morning and seeing her at the beach house as she was having her breakfast. He also loved to see her big smile and always said, "How is our Lucka Ducka doing today?" (Meaning, those were the few words she could say and repeatedly said it all day long) Marie then responded to my dad, "Luka Ducka." My dad would say to Marie, "You don't say. Is that right Marie? What else do you think?" Marie would smile and smile at her grandfather as she knew he adored her. My father always said to me, "Julie, Marie was sent to you for a reason, God only knows why and you just love her the best way you can and I know you will." He was right. I soon found out just how much we love her.

The summer came to a close and I was going back to work in the fall after having Joseph in January.

My sister was going to watch three babies, one of my younger sister's and two of mine—Joe and Marie. We had all the schedules worked out between myself and my younger sister Joan to bring her daughter to my house. We would wave good-bye and left my older sister Mary with the three kids, who were, by the way, all under three; two of them were infants. As I checked in each day most of the time, all hell would break loose and the three kids were on all different stages in life and driving Mary crazy. The sad part was we didn't even pay Mary so well. Steve and I were always broke and didn't have much money. Joan did pay Mary and well, I think that's why she really stayed and babysat for the three and she needed my house to work from. No, just kidding, she loved all the kids. Mary babysat all the grandchildren or at least seven of the eleven. I worked part time when I went back so Mary only had my kids three days a week. Mary did great with taking care of all the kids, and we were glad we didn't have to put them in day care.

It was Marie's first day of school and I was to put her on the bus, and she was going to be met at her new school by her tutor. Well, it was easier said than done. I panicked and called my supervisor who was also the special education director for our town and told her, "I can't put Marie on the bus. She is just too small to go to school by herself, I'm not doing it." The supervisor said to me, "Julie, get a grip. You have got to put Marie on that bus that is waiting in front of your house now!" She proceeded to tell me that I was just having separation anxiety and Marie will be fine. I then told her, "Okay! I will put her on the bus, but I'm not sure about this." It took me everything I had in me to put Marie on that bus but I did it.

Marie did go to school and had a great day, and I was so happy to see her come off that bus. I then had no problem sending her as she went to school each day. Marie did miss days from school due to seizures that she had during the night. Ninety-nine percent of Marie's seizures were happening at night, especially during her sleep. The preschool teacher was so great with Marie. They all enjoyed having her and included her in all the activities at school. Some days, I drove Marie to school. On the days I wasn't working, I dropped her off and picked her up. She had to be in a handicapped stroller and had a walker to get around with in school and at home. It just made things easier for me and Marie if I did the transporting some of the time. Marie got into her routine and the school year was a success for Marie and me.

It was March 29, 2003, and there was another benefit being planned by Steve's parents' friends Kim and Rick and Steve's mom and dad.

Marie was now almost four years old; she would be on May 21, 2003. She was still having her seizures, but we were able to control them at home with the help of Valium we kept on hand.

As the benefit came closer, we were receiving support from friends and family. I felt so thankful for all the kindness that everyone in our community was doing to help us. We went to the benefit and Marie was now four years old. Marie was overwhelmed by all the people who came to the benefit for her. There were friends from her school and her tutor had come also to see Marie. We, again, were so in shock from all the work and support given to have the benefit in Marie's behalf. Steve and I carried her around all night as she looked at everyone and soaked up all the love everyone had shown her. Marie became exhausted as the night went on, so we did finally have to bring her home.

I was told the employees at a local grocery store raised money for Marie's benefit by wearing jeans on Friday and donating money to a charity which happened to be Marie's benefit. A restaurant owner had donated food as his donation to Marie's benefit. People in the community gave gift baskets and raffle prizes for the benefit. The benefit was just amazing and we could not believe the kindness people had shown us. We felt a little awkward after having the first benefit which was given for us, but to have the generosity given to us again by friends was just amazing.

We again were backed up on our bills and expenses as Marie had had the brain surgery, and we had to miss so much time off from work and couldn't get caught up. I remember saying to Steve I hope my work doesn't find out about the benefit but they did. The school I worked at was always so kind and generous to me. I just didn't want them to do any more for my family. The school principal announced that the benefit was to be on the weekend when the time came and so they gave and gave once again.

We could never repay all our friends for giving the benefits and the kind support from the community. But I do keep trying to help people whenever I can. I truly believe in paying it forward. If someone does kindness for you, it is your obligation or moral responsibility to do unto others. The support from family and friends has also taught us a great lesson. There is always help at a time in your life when you need it most. In turn, as I have said, at any time you can be of help, you should; we owe it to people in the community who have helped us.

We need to help them to relieve their pain. I try to seek out families with handicapped members or people down on

47

their luck. I feel that so much was given to us that we need to help others whether it is in monetary ways, education or helping to collect for a food or clothing drive. I will keep trying to help others.

Having a child with a severe medical condition has taught our family to open our hearts and minds as we have seen the heartache people go through, not just having a handicapped child. We have seen what people go through by having a child so sick and die from an incurable disease. We have seen the pain from parents of babies in the hospital who hang on to life for the smallest pleasures they receive from their very sick child. My husband was visiting Marie in the hospital and came across an acquaintance who said he was visiting his son in the hospital also. My husband was complaining about something minor, I think something like we didn't sleep all night because Marie was having seizures. This acquaintance said to Steve, "Yeah, I'm waiting for my son's chemotherapy to start working." It wasn't helping cure his cancer so far. Steve said he felt so insensitive and like an idiot because this father had a real complaint about life and ours was so minor compared to what this dad was going through. Watching his son die in front of his eyes and there was nothing this dad could do to help him. We saw many parents go through many tragedies they had to overcome. You go into the children's hospitals and see children hooked up to ventilators in their wheelchairs or not able to move a muscle and they cannot speak and just stare out. You learn to be glad and appreciate what you have and feel sorry for the pain and sorrow those children have along with their parents. You see the heartbreak in the parents of these children as life is so difficult for them to care for their child. The pain you see in their eyes as they take care of their child so frail and weak. They get their joy and pleasure from their child when they achieve the smallest of tasks.

As Marie gets her beginning of education, we start to get ours. Not only from Marie but the world we are surrounded by. We are glad for the education for we would have never known this whole other world existed of disabled and handicapped or seriously ill children, if we had not been put in this world of Marie's. I would have probably gone through life with a closed mind and with blinders on had it not been for Marie coming into our life. I'm not saying, "Gee, I'm so glad Marie is such a sick child, but she has opened up our world to a whole different life." I can recall a friend and my supervisor giving me a great piece of advice. She told me that having a child like Marie, you need to go through a grieving period until I can understand and accept Marie's condition as death. I thought at first this was a harsh way to put her condition or life, but in reality, she could not have put it in better terminology for me to understand. She meant until I realized Marie will never be what I want her life to be. My unrealistic expectations will never be real until I could deal with Marie and that she will never be like any other little girl. I needed to see this myself and it did take me a long time to go through changing my way of thinking and to accept Marie for just the way she will always be. I did have to grieve as if I lost the daughter I thought I had. I had to come to the realization that she will never be normal. It was actually a relief when I really thought about it. I felt a weight had been lifted off my shoulders. I no longer had to find Marie's life to be perfect. I no longer longed for that little perfect daughter. I can look at Marie as my *special* daughter, and I love her with all my heart and soul just the way she is. I am so thankful I have her and love to see her with us each and every day. She is my little angel given to me from heaven and I look at her as a gift.

Dealing with School and Where to Go

In the fall of 2003, Marie began another year of preschool as we decided to keep her there one more year. Her teacher and the school staff thought it was best for Marie to stay in preschool another year. The beginning of school was a rough start for Marie since she was so sick. Her cold never seemed to go away and her fever was up. After a couple of weeks of her not feeling well, she ended up going to the hospital. I didn't make such a big deal of her being sick due to the fact I thought it was just a cold or flu and she would get better. Marie went into the hospital after she had spiked a high fever of 103 degrees. Marie was so ill; the hospital had brought in every specialist and every doctor to find out what was the matter with her. Poor Marie just lay in the hospital bed sleeping and never woke up. There was one intern who was adamant about getting an IV hooked up to Marie. The doctors and nurses had tried and tried but every vein was blown. What I mean by blown is, as the nurses explained to me, that every vein they could find had been used for IVs too much. They just couldn't get a vein to produce a good connection to draw blood out. Blood was still going through; they just couldn't access the veins for blood or to hook up an IV. So they moved Marie into another room. I was with her as they tried to get an IV into her and still couldn't. They must have stuck her ten times between her wrists, arms, legs and even her ankles. It was always a challenge to get blood or an IV outlet. Marie always was challenging for the hospital staff to get an IV into or draw blood from because she so frequently had to have blood drawn or because of being hospitalized so much her veins were tiny and so hard to locate. So now we were back to the days of trying to get an IV into her. They had poked her so much and she was screaming and crying because each time they had tried to prick her with the needle, it hurt so much. This one doctor or intern was so kind and he had called a nurse from intensive care who we knew and because she was the expert at getting IVs in. She tried and tried herself and finally said that she had to stop. There was no way she could get a line in. I, by this time, am trying to console Marie and hoping this agony will be over. The mean intern, as I called her, still insisted the IV had to get in. The intern was concerned that if Marie started having seizures, they wouldn't be able to get medication into her without an IV access, which I clearly understood her point. I then began getting really upset telling the intern, "We are stopping this right now. Marie can't handle the pain anymore and I won't have her going through this or let you do this to her." The doctor began telling me that if she has seizures what will we do then. My response was we could give her the Valium rectally as we do at home. I also explained to the intern that Marie won't have any more seizures she usually has her big bang seizures and then they stop as they did upon admittance to the hospital. This is how we ended up coming to the hospital is Marie's seizures came with high fever and we had brought her in by ambulance again. The intern finally agreed mostly because the nice intern had backed me up and said, "The mom is right. We can't do this anymore." When children are small, as I was told by nurses, their baby fat makes it difficult to reach veins and this was the case with Marie. So the two interns had said okay, let Marie have a break from the pain and let her go back to her room. We did go back and I had to now deal with the pressure on myself and hope this baby doesn't have a seizure. I just had a fit with the intern and told her nothing would happen to Marie. They even made me sign a form saying I am responsible if anything should occur. It was in my hands and I released the hospital of any wrongdoing, (so no pressure on me at all!). Marie continued to be so ill and weak after the entire trauma she just went through with the IV incident. I finally called one of the doctors who was in the group of Marie's pediatricians and explained to him how I thought it was just a sinus infection that just went terribly wrong. I had begged this doctor to put her on antibiotics after I had asked another one of Marie's pediatricians to give her an antibiotic and he wouldn't. Well, I asked the second pediatrician. I had called him up and really begged him to give her an antibiotic just to try to see if she comes around. Marie had always had sinus problems anyway and antibiotics always cleared them. So this doctor finally agreed to give Marie the antibiotics as a trial to see if it would help her. We were on day two of nothing being done to help her. The minute I got off the phone and a nurse came in, I was so happy to ask her if she received the orders for the antibiotic the pediatrician agreed to. The nurse said she didn't get the orders but would find out. Two or three hours went by and I was now calling Steve at home screaming about not getting the antibiotics and if he could call the doctor. Steve had told me to calm down, of course, because I was always nuts when it came to Marie. He said the orders for the antibiotic will come. After about three hours, the nurse finally came in with the antibiotics. Marie just slept and her fever was still up, and during the night, she even spiked to 105 degrees. Around seven in the morning, the doctors all started coming in and said they just didn't know what was wrong with Marie, and I began to give them my theory of how I thought she had a sinus infection that I just let go too long. Well, one of them said, "I don't know. She's pretty sick and there are no nasal fluids coming out of her, so we don't think so."

The infection control specialist doctors came in and saw Marie again and checked her over and over. They had said, "We would have to agree with her mom. It is probably a sinusitis that's just making her so ill." I didn't even know what sinusitis was. I was just so happy they found a diagnosis for Marie. They said to leave her on the antibiotics and see how she does. I then asked one of Marie's pediatricians when they came in, "What is sinusitis?" The doctor then told me, "It's a sinus infection." I was so glad because I was still holding my breath believing everyone thought I was completely nuts at this point. I then proceeded to call my husband and tell him that I'm not crazy and Marie has a sinus infection. Steve was in his glory to finally have an answer to why Marie was so sick, and also he now knew that they could cure this illness.

Marie finally started to react to the antibiotics after two or three doses, she was waking up and alert. Her fever had dropped and she was up in my arms eating and drinking and doing well.

The doctors let Marie go and rest at home. In a week, she was back in school. While Marie was back at preschool, things were going fine. She was working with the therapist and getting involved with her classmates at school. She received so much attention from everyone and they were all happy to have her there.

Life was going well for Marie and things seemed normal for a while until more trouble was brewing right under my nose it seemed. What transpired next, I had no idea what was coming and life at school was going to be so difficult. Marie had a new teacher since the one who agreed to keep her back went on to another grade.

I didn't know the new teacher but figured she would be fine with Marie. The new teacher had called me at the beginning of the year and told me how she knew so much about handicapped children, and she went to college for special education which was her major.

Anyway, we chatted and she seemed nice and everything seemed to be fine. The trouble had started when I was at my sister's hair salon, getting a haircut for my son Joseph. Marie was out of school so much the last few weeks, and in the hospital, I couldn't even find the time to get Joe's haircut. So anyway, I was about to put Joe in the chair—Joe is three at this time—when I got a call from the school. My sister picked up the phone and the school said that I needed to go and get Marie as she was messy. I immediately grabbed Joe and run to the school.

I arrived at the school within ten minutes from the call and I walked into Marie's classroom. The therapists were all working with Marie and doing their usual workout or therapy. The tutor came up to me and said, "Mrs. Fargo, what are you doing here? Is everything all right?" I said to her, "What do you mean? Someone here called me and said I needed to come and pick up Marie. She was messy or something like that." The tutor went over and explained to the entire therapist staff what I was doing there and they responded, "We didn't call you. Marie is fine. You can leave her. She just had a bowel movement that was messy, but we cleaned her up and she's fine." I looked at Marie and she looked very happy to be there and then said to the therapist, "Then why did you call me and tell me to come pick her up." One of the therapists then went over to the teacher and asked if she had called me. She, just in passing, because she was with other students said, "I called the mom because she needs to take Marie home and give her a bath. She's a mess." The therapist said, "No, she doesn't. Marie is all cleaned up and she is okay, we are working with Marie." The teacher just shot me a look like get her out so I turned to the therapist and said, "I am taking Marie home. How dare anyone tell me I need to take my kid home and give her a bath. I take very good care of her and practically bathe her every day." With that remark, I took Joe and Marie out of the school and was so upset I just couldn't believe someone telling me to take my daughter out of school because she had a messy bowel movement. I had said I think this isn't the way we are going to go all year because if so, it will be a long year.

I received a phone call from Marie's teacher later in the afternoon when school was out for the day. The teacher proceeded to tell me why she called me and told me to take Marie home after her incident at school. I had explained to the teacher I had heard her point, that it stunk in the class and it wasn't necessary for the other children to have to tolerate Marie's stinky bowel movement. But I told the teacher she was so rude and insulting about the situation. I had told her she could have come up to me upon my arrival and explained the situation and I would have understood. She instead ignored me and never told anyone that she had called me. We continued to go back and forth, and I admit I became very rude to her. I think the general gist of the conversation went something to the effect of that, "She, the teacher, had no business being involved with special ed children because she had no knowledge of how to deal with them or their family, and that these type of problems may arise, and she better figure out how to handle situations better and in a more sensitive manner if she plans on staying in special ed and with handicapped children." Before I could shut up, I realized I had upset her and she was crying, which I never wanted to do. I had just been through the ordeal of Marie being in the hospital and just didn't need another problem this week. We hung up and both the teacher and I never did resolve anything except we were both stuck on our point. I believe she ended hanging up saying she is fully qualified and will continue on her ways of doing things. The only other problem I had with the situation was she is also Joe's teacher as he goes to the same preschool in the morning. She is great with Joe but he is not in special ed so she loves him.

I cooled off and brought Marie back to school on Monday as the incident had happened on a Friday afternoon. I stayed clear of the teacher from there since the tutor picked up Marie and went with her on the bus as she did everyday now. So life went on and things seemed to calm down until about a month later, Marie ended up in the hospital for seizures and we had a rough weekend with her. Marie had to be admitted to the hospital I believe for another illness but was home in a day.

Marie came out of the hospital and I was dropping off Joseph for preschool, and the teacher came up to me and said she needed to talk to me. I left Joe with his classmates and she said, "From now on when Marie is not coming to school, the school needs to be called by 7:30 a.m." I was in such shock. I didn't know what to think. I had to be at my dentist in five minutes so I really didn't have time to get into a discussion or find out what happened to bring this new rule on. Granted, Marie had been out off and on, and she would have a seizure, not too often, but if she was ill, her seizures would sometimes start in the morning, so we couldn't send her to school and would call. Sometimes it was last minute or right before she was to go in. We couldn't control that. I went home after my dentist's appointment and called Marie's tutor. I was still in a huff and upset about the teacher telling me to call at 7:30 a.m. Anyway, the tutor said, "I can't believe she approached you about that matter. I asked her to please wait and talk to you in a few days because you had just come out of the hospital with Marie. "I told her I didn't understand. As long as they have somewhere to send the tutor in Marie's absence, which they did, what's the problem?" I then called the principal and said I needed to speak to her. She said that I would have to come in to talk to her. I grabbed Joe and went to the principal's office. I just started to cry and was so upset. The principal knew at this point this was going to be hard on Joe so, she grabbed some toys and had him play outside her office with the secretary watching him. I then began telling her what was going on and how the teacher had been. I thought she at this point was prejudiced or had something against Marie and was going to make her life at school a living hell. This teacher didn't really have to deal with Marie. Marie had a tutor who did everything, so I wasn't sure what the problem was. All I could conclude is Marie's special needs were a threat or she just didn't want to have to deal with this kid. This was not what she had bargained for as a teacher. The principal had told me she was aware of the problem and said they just needed more notice in the morning so they could know what to do with the tutor for the afternoon. The tutor was only part-time and an assistant tutor, so she could only work with kids on a part-time basis and the need for her was not there if Marie wasn't in school. I told her in so many words, I don't buy that because they never had a problem placing her with a student before. I know they usually back up the teacher as I work in a school and know how the system works; they're certainly not going to admit the teacher was wrong besides the teacher's family was big and influential in our town. So I left again with no answers and went home still steamed about the whole situation again.

I talked to the tutor once I got home and told her, and she said she was getting tired of the teacher, too. The teacher had apparently been barking orders at the tutor for some time and always tried to control her by not letting her do activities with Marie or telling her she wasn't doing things she was suppose to with Marie. After talking to the tutor, I called the principal that day and told her, "I wouldn't be sending Marie to school anymore if this teacher doesn't want her there. I don't want Marie in an environment where she isn't welcomed or liked. She told me to please bring her back, this won't be a problem and not to worry. I had calmed down and said I would send her.

Marie then had seizures and couldn't go to school so I called at 7:30 a.m. There was no answer, and of course, there was no one at the school since school doesn't begin until 8:46 a.m. Well, I kept trying and eventually either left a message or got a secretary, I'm not sure. The tutor had showed up at my house that morning to pick up Marie. I told her Marie's not going to school and I had already called the school. No one informed the tutor, so she went to the school and they said, "Yes, they forgot to tell her." I sent Marie the next day and things were okay. *Things were back to normal*, I thought. I called in again, maybe it was a day or two later and our system failed again, the tutor wasn't called. We were told that communication was not to exist between the tutor and myself because it was against policy, and so, I wasn't suppose to call her and they also didn't like us talking and the tutor was not supposed to discuss with me anything of relevance to the school. Well, that didn't fly because I would call her to let her know when Marie would be out so she would know of her absence. This went on for a while and the teacher wasn't too nice to the tutor and continued to tell her how to take care of Marie. Finally, I said, enough. I called the principal. I had explained how I felt. That I didn't think Marie belongs at school any longer, and I wanted her moved out to a private school. I went in and had a meeting with all the school staff and town special education staff. We had decided Marie would go to a special school and we would start looking. The letters all went out and we were given a list of schools we could visit. We then started our search.

The next week, my husband and I went all over the state and looked at each school. We went to the first which was nice but was all special ed children in one class in this school. The staff was very nice but it just seemed so gloomy and Marie would be so far from home.

There were no children like Marie. She was only four years old and would be five in a month, but it just seemed she was too little to be that far way. The school was about a half an hour away and we had to go on the highway just to get there. If she had a seizure, she would have to go to the nearest hospital which was not the children's hospital and also it was too far away for us to get to. Steve had said, "No, she is not going there." To which I agreed.

We then, the next day, talked to another two of the schools and the administrator told us they don't take children as handicapped as Marie is.

So we took another ride to another school that was nearby in the next town. It was like a regular school and everyone was so nice. We were told that they do not allow nurses to come with the students as they have their own. We were thinking of and also in the process of getting a nurse for Marie, so we weren't happy with this news. We took a tour with one of the administrators and the school was great. We looked around though and just couldn't picture our little Marie here. The kids were from the age maybe eight to twenty-one years old. Marie was so small. Again, we just couldn't see her there either. So we walked out and we both said, "Well, that's not happening either, she can't go here."

I began calling some of the other schools we were told to visit and didn't like the age of the kids that I was told to go there. They were all so much older than our Marie. I asked them to send me tapes and an information packet of their schools. After receiving the tapes and pamphlets, I started to watch the tapes and couldn't see Marie fit in these schools either. They were as it seemed so institutionalized. Maybe they weren't but I just couldn't get there. I had heard good and bad stories from people who knew of these schools and researched all of them.

We came to the conclusion we couldn't do it. We would have to go back to the school Marie went to with our heads down and admit we couldn't send her to any of those schools. The school was very nice about our situation and agreed to let Marie stay there. We also agreed since her annual meeting was due that I would pick out her teacher for the next year (as I was advised by our case worker for the state). We had the meeting. The meeting went well. The school introduced us to a new teacher Marie would have for kindergarten and her present teacher was also there. The kindergarten teacher was very nice and sweet, and I knew right away she was going to be great. I did tell everyone at the meeting that I would not put up with any of the nonsense I had this year, and I just couldn't put us through that again. We all agreed that things would be better next year.

We went home and Marie went back to school and things were the same. The tutor had said she was quitting and didn't want to come back the following year as this year was too difficult for her. The tutor loved Marie but I certainly understood no job is worth going through the crap she had to endure in this year.

We were thinking about getting a nurse as I said before but put it on the back burner because it was not a priority now.

I received a phone call from the nurse at school saying how they put Marie on the bus but she didn't seem okay. They weren't sure what was going on with her. She had been making weird facial expressions and seemed in a daze. I then told the nurse to let her go on the bus because the traffic at the school would slow me down trying to get to her. So Marie came home with the tutor and as I looked at her, I could tell she was having a seizure. I told the tutor that Marie was having a seizure and I needed to get her in the house to give her Valium. I ran upstairs with her in my arms to Marie's bedroom where I could lay her down and inject the Valium. The tutor went home and I waited for Marie to come to, but she wasn't responding to the Valium. My mother-in-law was with me and we both were just standing over her bed and waited. Thirty minutes went by and nothing of a response from Marie, so we waited another thirty minutes and I finally said, "I'm calling the ambulance. She's not going to stop seizing." I could hear the ambulance sirens coming, and once again, my heart dropped as I was worried for Marie. The neighbors always knew it was for Marie as they watched me once again carry Marie out to the ambulance to put her on a stretcher. My mother and father-in-law stayed with Joe. My husband was coming home from work and heard the sirens from the police cars and ambulance and knew it was once again for Marie. Steve jumped out of his car, and I quickly told him she was seizing and we're going to the hospital. We went and Steve met us there. We watched the doctors and nurses worked on her. They immediately knew what to expect as they always said, "Oh! It's Marie, let's get to work." They proceeded to pump antiseizure meds into her. If I remember correctly, I believe she had an ear infection and that's why she was having such a terrible seizure. The doctors and nurses were able to get Marie to stop the seizures. The doctors had said before that you can have an ear infection and not have a fever, so I didn't know she had an ear infection. It probably began possibly from one of her sinus problems. She always had sinus problems. Having sinus problems for handicapped kids was highly common as they can't get rid of the fluid in the nasal passage because you can't get them to blow their nose.

Marie was feeling better as we were allowed to take her home with antibiotics to treat her ear infection. I was so stunned because she would usually cry or show she was in pain from her ear infections. She never had ear infections as a baby but developed them as she got older.

So Marie was back at home recovering from her ear infection and doing well. We then realized we really need a nurse to go to school with her as her seizures are starting to get out of control again.

The school nurse was very good as far as knowing Marie and she was very attentive to Marie's needs. The nurse did also have a whole school of children to take care of. We also had scared the tutor a little as this was our second or third tutor. Marie had been too much to handle for the others. One just said Marie made her too nervous and the other could not carry Marie. Going through tutors is a whole other story that I didn't tell because it would be too long and probably very boring to explain. It was also not the tutor's job to take care of Marie while having seizures, we barely knew what to do. We needed to find a nurse for Marie to have at school.

But before I finish, I have to tell you the conclusion of Marie's tutor's story that she had throughout the year—the tutor who had had a difficult year with the teacher. Well, as the end of the year approached, she told the school in writing and signed a paper which stated what each tutor wanted to do for their position in the next year. I know because I was a tutor at another school and had to ask for my position in the next year also. We had a new supervisor, so things were done a little differently. Anyway, Marie's tutor wrote down she did not want to come back the following school year. I was heartbroken because I really liked her and she cared so much for Marie like she was her own daughter and I trusted her. She would take Marie off the bus and when I looked at her, I could see she was upset and about to cry as she said good-bye to Marie. It makes me want to cry now as I think of the heart-wrenching decision she had made. She just turned to me and said, "I can't say good-bye to her. I really want to stay and be her tutor next year, I should not have quit." I said, trying to relieve her sadness and regret, "Don't feel sad. You can always come over and see Marie. She is not going anywhere." My words were not too consoling but the tutor did leave Marie and went home. We had talked on the phone throughout the summer. The tutor expressed to me on occasion how she wanted her job back and I had asked the principal but the answer was no. I even went in to see the principal of the school to see if I could get the tutor back not only for her sake, I have to admit, I was thinking of how it would be nice to have her back with Marie in the fall. The principal had quick flashed the letter in front of me and said, "Julie, she signed a letter stating the fact she did not want to come back to work in the fall." I soon left the principal's office and could no longer do anything about this situation. Just another thing to add to the great school year we had. Life was getting tougher as we were learning life was going to be a battle, and we always had to be prepared to fight for Marie no matter what it took.

I never knew I could be so aggressive and outspoken. I was learning to speak up and not be afraid to say anything for fear I may offend someone, like I used to. My husband was constantly telling me how aggressive I was and how I wasn't afraid to speak my mind. I only spoke my mind when it came to a problem dealing with Marie. Anything else, I didn't worry about the small stuff. You could pretty much still walk all over me but when, like I said, it came to Marie or Joe, don't toy with me. I'm usually not in the mood and usually upset enough to tell people off as needed.

After having such a wonderful day, I had just put Marie down for the night and Steve was going out with his friends. Joe was playing on the porch and I could hear him playing as I was listening to him and washing dishes. A police officer showed up and I saw the police car in my driveway. The police officer came up to my porch as I could see him and talked to him from my window. Well, anyway, the police officer asked me, "Is Marie all right?" I said to him, "Yes, Marie is fine." He then explained to me, "We received a 911 call from your house and I came right over thinking Marie was having trouble." I said to him, "Marie is fine. I didn't call 911." He then said, "Are you sure? We definitely received the call." I said, "Yes, of course. I'm sure. I did not call 911." I went in to check to see what Joe was really up to and he had the phone right next to him and when I asked, "Joe, were you on the phone? He looked pretty guilty but not sure what he was guilty of. Joe's answer to my question was "Yes, Mommy. I was talking on the phone." I said to the police officer as he was still in my doorway trying to figure out what was going on, "I'm sorry to make you come out. My son must have called dialing numbers on the phone." The officer knew me well enough and took my word for it that everything was okay and he then left.

Joe was about two years old at this stage. I told Joe after that he couldn't play with the phone and I was so tired I didn't really want to get into the *whys* with my two-year-old and just had to laugh it off. Never a dull moment in our house even when I think I have everything under control. There always seems to be something brewing. Sometimes, we are thankful for the things in life we can look back and laugh at, and this was one and everyone was fine.

Time to Find a Nurse

Marie was now five years old and going into kindergarten. We adjusted her schedule so she would go to school later because she had seizures during the night and slept late to recover from the seizures. We did call a few agencies to find a nurse and found out Marie's insurance would give her one full time. The problem was going to find a competent and a good nurse. My mother often told me I was looking for Mary Poppins and to be careful. I was not going to find her. That was so true. Well, my expectations were high, I have to admit, but what was to come down the pike, I had no idea. We called one agency and they said they would send out a nurse the following day. The next day came and this nurse showed up at 8:00 a.m. as she was told to by the agency, which was fine. I had a dog, a Dalmatian, who barked and barked at her when she came in. I finally had to throw my dog outside to stop him from killing her. She looked like someone who came out of the sixties and liked the eighties look too. She had sneakers that were worn, spandex pants with socks that were wrapped from her ankles to her knees, eyes that were so bloodshot, and hair that was long and hadn't been brushed in a few days. I introduced her to Marie and I explained how to take care of Marie. The nurse was having a difficult time following my direction. She proceeded to tell me she would have to leave early because she had a heart condition and a seizure disorder herself. I said, "Sure, that's fine. You can leave early today." I'm thinking, real early, sweetheart. You're on the next bus out. She then continued to tell me about her personal life, which was not a happy story. She told me among other things, of how her husband is in jail in a maximum security prison and doing time for a crime she wouldn't say. *Thank God for that*, I thought. She then asked if I minded if she went to smoke outside and she did. We then tried after to get Marie ready and to put her on the bus. I had to put Marie on the bus and called the school and said the nurse was not going with her today. Marie went to school and everything was okay. The nurse had said she would be back after her doctor's appointment—with her heart doctor, great. This nurse came back at 3:00 to meet Marie coming off the bus. This new nurse went to the bus smoking a cigarette and had the cigarette hanging from her mouth to get Marie off the bus. I thought to myself, *Don't drop the cigarette on my kid getting off the bus, just keep smoking, sweetheart! You idiot, you're so gone.* The bus driver who I had known for years of taking Marie to school had turned to me, and I'll never forget her face when she said, "Julie, you can't be serious about this! That nurse is awful." I then told her not to worry. This is her first and last day. She's gone today. The nurse came in with Marie and I looked at her. She looked either stoned or drunk. Her eyes were so bloodshot and she was flying around the house like a mad woman. She had told me she took medications. I don't know for what, but she seemed like she was really enjoying whatever meds she was on. I told her I could handle things from here and good-bye. She said, "I'll see you tomorrow." I thought, *Yeah, sure you will. You're high as a kite and I'm going to let you be with my daughter another day?* When Steve came home from work, I told him all about the nurse and he said, "Give her another chance. You're just being overprotective." Steve was very protective of Marie too. I think he really couldn't believe there were nurses like that out there. So I tried to sleep that night. I slept on it and tried to think on a positive side, but I couldn't find any. The next morning, after not sleeping, I got up at 5:30 a.m. and told Steve I was calling the agency and telling them not to send that nurse back out. At 7:00 a.m. I called the agency and told the supervisor not to send her out to my house again. He then asked me, "What's the problem?" I then said to him, "Are you kidding me? If you think I didn't see that woman for what she is." I told him she did more drugs than my daughter, and my daughter is in better shape than the nurse was." I then was yelling by then at what an idiot he was. I also told him that she had told me that her husband was in a federal maximum security jail for twenty years for what I didn't know or care. He asked me if she told me all that. I said, "Yes, along with stories of the rest of her ridiculous life." I also told him how the bus driver even told me not to keep her and how she went out to the bus smoking a cigarette. I had also told him how I knew someone who knew her and she had a terrible reputation. He then asked me to give the agency another chance and let them send out another nurse to which I said yes. I had to work so I was desperate to find someone to take care of Marie. I had missed so much work due to Marie being out or being called at work to go home because an ambulance was on the way to help Marie with seizures. The secretaries and teachers in my work eventually became so tired of trying to find me in the building and told me that I had to carry my cell phone. Well, anyway, I let the agency send a new nurse.

She came the following day and I was off work so I could stay with her all day.

So when she came in, she was a little rough around the edges to say the least. She was a young nurse in her twenties. She had a little boy with seizures and she began to tell me about it. She said she couldn't leave the boy who was four years old with his father because his father wouldn't care for him. She barely spoke to Marie. She was more interested in my animals—my cats and dogs. She proceeded to tell me how she just rescued a litter of cats, but she couldn't pay her mortgage and was going to lose her home. I then gave her some cat food so she could have some food for these cats. She was grateful and I think she was so wrapped up in her own life she couldn't think of anyone else. I showed her what Marie needed and explained how to do things. This nurse never spoke to Marie and that really bothered me and I couldn't get past it. I let her go home and told her I'll see her tomorrow. I took Marie to school when I had off and was home with Joe.

The next day came and I asked my mother-in-law to come over and watch this new nurse as I didn't trust her. The day went on and my mother-in-law showed her what to do and helped her with Marie. When I came home, Marie was home that day because she slept late and couldn't wake up as she had a tough night with seizures we didn't even see. When I asked the new nurse if Marie had eaten at all throughout the day, she claimed Marie didn't want to eat and that she offered food once but Marie wouldn't eat. I thought okay that happens, sometimes Marie doesn't eat. When she left, my mother-in-law said she thought she was okay for a nurse and thought she could handle the job. I asked her if she spoke to Marie and she said a little. I went to check the report she wrote for the day. As I grabbed water from the refrigerator, I found out that the food I left for Marie was not even opened, so she could not have tried to feed Marie. My mother-in-law was busy taking care of Joe, too, so she couldn't watch everything the new nurse was doing. Then I checked the report she left for her agency and she wrote in it that Marie had a seizure. Well, she never mentioned that to me. I wasn't really trying to find something wrong with her as I have been accused by friends and even Steve. Really, I needed a nurse more than they needed me. Nurses were in demand and they knew it. After telling my husband I can't deal with this one either, I called the agency to fire her, too. "She didn't even say good-bye to Marie when she left." I told my husband. Steve thought I was being too hard on her and to give her and myself a break. I insisted on firing her and called the agency that afternoon. I explained to the agency what I thought was wrong and told them she was another incompetent nurse and had no personality and had too many problems of her own. The supervisor again listened to me and asked if he could send someone else out to which I said, "No, I'm finished with the nurses from his agency."

I then called another agency and they agreed to send a supervising nurse out to set up and go over the paperwork. The supervisor came the next morning and did the paperwork with me. The new agency sent out another nurse the following week on Monday. This nurse was very friendly and looked completely normal. She told me she had been a trauma nurse at a children's hospital. She was great! I explained all our needs and she just fit in perfectly, loved Marie and had such enthusiasm. I couldn't believe how great she was. I remember leaving her right away and going to the grocery store and not worrying for the first time in a long time about caring for Marie. I came back from the grocery store and she came out and helped me with the groceries. Marie was down for a nap, as I noticed on the monitor when I came in. We talked and she told me how she was getting married the next summer and she had three kids. Everything was great; she came back in a couple of days as she could only work part-time with Marie because she had another case she didn't like because it was in a really tough neighborhood in another town. When she came back the next time, everything went well. I could drop Joe off at his preschool and then go to my job.

I came home from work and Marie came home from school with the nurse and the bus driver said, "This one's a keeper, Julie." About the nurse she meant. Marie looked good and everything went well. What a relief, we finally had a good nurse.

I was about to go to work but received a call from the nursing agency. The supervisor had told me that our new nurse was in a car accident. I quickly asked her if the nurse was okay, and she said yes but has a broken leg and would be in the hospital with cuts and bruises and pretty banged up. She also said she would be in a cast for six to eight weeks. I, then, like an idiot asked, "Well, is she coming back after that?" To which the supervisor informed me, "No, she wouldn't be. She is getting married in the summer and is due to go on her honeymoon." So I proceeded to ask her, "Well, could I talk to her or get in touch with her?" The supervisor had again told me that right now she is in the hospital and hurting and didn't think it was possible to contact her. I was desperate I think. I felt now, "The hell with her injuries." I wanted Marie's nurse back. All I could think of was she was perfect.

"What am I going to do now?" The agency said they would look for a new nurse for Marie. "I didn't want a new nurse." I told my husband. I wanted that nurse back as I whined to him all night. He said we can find another nurse.

A couple of weeks went by and there was no nurse. The agency didn't have anyone to send to us. The school year was ending and summer was almost here. It was April when the agency called and they said they had another nurse and would send her out the next day.

The next nurse came out again at 8:00 a.m. She seemed nice but a little strange. What I mean is she asked so many questions about things that just should be common sense. She asked me where the book was that the nurses chart everything or write down all their notes. I gave her the book and she wanted to go over every detail of why the previous nurse wrote down such things. I told her I didn't know much about what the nurses were told to write, but she was welcome to change what she wanted. She took Marie's temperature every hour it seemed and let us be aware what it was every hour, which to be honest, we didn't really give a crap as long as she didn't have a fever. So I began showing her where things were and how to do things. But she just did not let up on the smallest detail. The details I mean were why did we have a lift in place and not have it fully set up yet in her room. Which I guess wasn't as bizarre as we explained we were told by a physical therapist that we should get this as Marie will use it when she gets bigger. She just couldn't understand it. She went through all Marie's drawers and couldn't understand why we put clothes in there or how we put clothes in her dresser. She was nice to

Marie and I knew she would take care of her, but she just nitpicked at everything. She kept calling the agency and asked them questions and constantly wanted the records in order. She did more taking care of the books and measured the medicine about twenty times before she gave it to Marie. This nurse kept telling us that her temperature was ninety-nine or a hundred degrees auxiliary. We didn't even know what auxiliary meant, but we were so sick of hearing about it all the time. This nurse drove the agency crazy as they had to keep calling her back or come out to our house for the most smallest of issues she made. So after about ten days, I had to call the agency and tell them I couldn't take her anymore; she was driving me crazy with her notes and temperature readings and she never stopped talking. The agency understood and actually told me she was driving them crazy, too. She apparently worked the night shift at a group home and wasn't so accustomed to dealing with people all day. She was a nervous lady and couldn't, as I said, do her job and keep quiet. So that was the end of her.

The agency was looking again for a new nurse, and we joked a lot about the previous nurse as they knew not to send another nurse like her. They called me up again after a week went by and said they had a new nurse for us and would be sending her out the next day or two. They would let me know. The agency called back the next day and said the new nurse was coming out tomorrow.

The next day, the new nurse arrived at 8:00 a.m. I had the day off so I could show her how to do things for Marie. She was an older woman and very pleasant. She said the only thing that would hold her back from taking Marie as a patient was she wasn't sure if she could lift Marie. Marie was now five and going to turn six years old in a couple of weeks. Marie only weighed thirty pounds as she wasn't gaining weight and was very tall. The new nurse Joan now tried carrying her as we did all around the house. Joan was not having trouble picking her up and was able to carry her up and down the stairs. She was great. She fit in perfectly with Marie and cared for her so well. She was so courteous and just loved Marie. Joan worried about her when she wasn't with her and just was a blessing from God. We thought finally we found a nurse and she was staying for good.

To be honest, I can't recall Joan going to school with Marie. I don't think she did. I think she got her ready for school and put her on the bus and went home. Marie was now in kindergarten and had a new tutor at school that was really nice.

There were three or four nurses hired as I look at the books with nurse's notes. I didn't want to bore you with all the details but they came and left. One, I now remember, left to take a full-time job with benefits as the agencies usually did not give benefits to the nurses. Another left after two months; she was due to have her baby. Another nurse came for orientation and disclosed to me she couldn't lift since she was expecting a child in seven months, but didn't tell the agency. The reasons were not just because of me being overprotective and I had to keep an open mind to each nurse who came through our home.

Nurse Joan began to work for us in May 2004 and things were finally going well. As I said, Marie had a great tutor and a wonderful, kind, and caring teacher. Marie was walking in her little walker and loved to watch all the colorful walls at school as she walked in the hallway. Marie still missed days from school due to seizures but went as often as she could.

Things Are Going Too Smooth

On September 25, 2004, Marie had come home with a note in her backpack from another parent at school. In the note was an invitation to a birthday party for a little girl in Marie's class. The note went into great details of how this parent would like to have Marie come to her daughter's birthday party. The mom said she was a special education teacher and was so experienced with children with special needs. Anyway, she said she would like Marie to come to her daughter's party and how her daughter loves Marie. I did hear that this little girl was attached to Marie at school and enjoyed being around Marie. The mother asked me to call if I would like Marie to come to this birthday party. I replied and spoke to the mother of the little girl and said Marie would love to come, but Marie could only stay a little while as it is difficult for her. A couple of weeks go by and it is Saturday, October 3 and the day of the birthday party for the little girl in Marie's kindergarten class. I got Marie all dressed in a pretty dress and had her hair all done up and she looked so beautiful. I wrapped the gift and ran out the door with Marie to the party. I found the address of the party as I pulled in the driveway. The little girl's dad came out and said hello and asked me if I needed help, to which I said, "No, I am used to carrying Marie. I'm fine."

The father was very polite and asked me to come in the house as the other little girls were already there for the party, and then he told the mother we were there. The mom approached and introduced herself; her daughter, whom the birthday party was for, came over at the mother's request and said hello to Marie. The mom then told me to go in; the girls were all having certain stations to get their hair, nails, and makeup done. So I said, "Oh, won't that be fun!" They were also doing arts and crafts. The mom told me where every station was and to do what I would think Marie would like to do. I then sat at this big long table with Marie on my lap and started doing a craft project which was almost impossible with Marie on my lap. I finished the craft project and all the little girls at the party were doing their own thing. The mom was getting her hair done and playing with the girls at the party. The mom's sister then asked me if Marie would like her nails done after. I said, "Sure, that would be fun." As I'm about to carry Marie over to the station to get her nails done, another little girl announced she was next and went to sit down to wait for her turn. I am still sitting there with Marie and all the little girls at the party run outside to play and the mom said they could go. Meanwhile, the mother was busy getting herself all made up and didn't speak to me or Marie the whole time we were there. The mother of the little girl just completely ignored us like we were not even there. She was just sitting there doing her thing. The aunt of this little girl asked me again if Marie would like her nails done. I said sure, still trying to keep my head up and feeling like I'm drowning and no one will help rescue me. I'm feeling like a complete outcast as no one was bothering with us. The girls were all out playing; the mom's not even telling her daughter to pay any attention to Marie at all. I could understand Marie couldn't go out and run around with them but not one girl came up and spoke to Marie. They just went about their business as if Marie didn't exist. The dad did ask us if we would like a burger since he was making them for the girls. I said no thank you, thinking to be polite but I couldn't very well eat while holding Marie. Yes, I could have brought her stroller in the house but not sure it would fit in their house and it might be awkward to make the family try to accommodate her stroller. I did think about bringing the stroller in but couldn't be inconspicuous about it. We moved over to get Marie's nails done and I'm trying to make light of the situation but feeling pretty awkward. The aunt was very nice and asked me all about Marie and what was wrong with her and she told me about her work she did. The aunt who was doing Marie's nails was very nice and I think she knew how awkward I felt because after we were done, I just sat there not sure what to do next. No one was around the room at all now. We seemed to have evacuated everyone. By now, the mom was gone and I never saw her around either. The next thing I knew, the girls came in from outside and the mom yelled, "Time for pizza!" To which I think, *Oh good. This should be fun. Marie will enjoy this.* So we're sitting there and the mom said, "Would Marie like some pizza?" I replied, "No, thank you. She's fine." The girls were all sitting around the table and still not one came over and spoke to Marie when they came in. I then said, "We have to be going. Thank you very much for the party." The mom did show me to the front door and asked her daughter to come say good-bye to Marie, but she couldn't because she was too busy eating and I told her, "That's okay." The mom grabbed a goody bag for Marie and we thank her and left. I just got Marie in her car seat and just wanted to cry for her. I felt so sad for Marie that she was so left out. All I could think of was and say to myself was it's just me and you (meaning, Marie against the world); no one understands her world.

I got home, carried Marie in the house and I couldn't open my mouth to tell Steve how sad I felt for myself and Marie. I told Steve I should have never gone and that was the first party Marie went to and the last. I told Steve how the mother just completely ignored us and how she portrayed herself to be such an expert with special education children. Well, I guess her idea of ignore or just stick your nose up in the air was how you deal with special education children. I went from sad to mad in two seconds and wanted to call the mother up and tell her if she had any experience and any kind of knowledge of special needs kids she certainly did not show it. Most of all, I think she was just a snob and carried on about her daughter as if she was a little princess and said how wonderful the little snot was all the time (no jealousy there!). Seriously, I really felt she was so rude and any adult would know better than she did as far as how to deal with the situation. I think she did know but she had the attitude of I'm better than you and want to show it. I learned in life that those people will stare you down and maybe laugh, but I feel sorry for them now because I know they have not really achieved anything or know anything about life or people. I could have been one like her but really don't think so. She was just so ignorant. I don't envy people like her. I just try to avoid them now as they do not do anything substantial in life and really have narrow-minded objectives. How was that for how do you really feel? Well, Steve did tell me something when I came home. He said, "I thought that might happen if you went to that party." He felt terrible for both of us. I vowed I would never take Marie to another party ever again so as not put her through it again or myself.

Marie went back to school on Monday as if nothing ever happened. I think the little girl still talked to Marie and was her friend. I'm really not sure why the little girl was friendly with Marie at school but couldn't be bothered when she had her friends around. I'm really not being sarcastic. I really didn't know what to make of it but figured I have bigger worries and to move on. Marie continued on with her daily life and things went back to the way they were. We had a great nurse for Marie now, so we were happy and content with life.

Marie was going through life as best she could and doing her routine that she had been so accustomed to. November went by with nothing to really point out but December was a little more of a struggle. It was December 22, 2005, and Marie started having seizures that were really intense and we couldn't stop with Valium at home. I had to call 911 for an ambulance to come and take her to the children's hospital. She was not responding and we were afraid to drive her in case she couldn't breathe. We got to the hospital and again the doctors and nurses realize its Marie and start putting her in the emergency room right away and started working on her to stop the seizures. The nurses were trying to get the IV in again as it was usually a challenge. Finally, they got the IV in after a couple of tries. Thank God, because as I said that is always the big problem for Marie. The nurse now tried to get the medication in and nothing was working. She was still seizing, so the doctor instructed them to give her more medication. Finally, the second dose worked and Marie stopped seizing. It had been two to three hours since she started seizing and she was calm. We then went up to a room, so they could keep a watch on her. The doctor can't find anything physically wrong with her. She needed to be watched as we were told. Marie slept through the night and woke up screaming and really hyperactive as she often did when she had a large amount of medication. She then started having seizures again and the nurses had to give her medication to get her out of the seizures she was having. The neurologist decided to give her another type of medication to see if this would help. Marie started to get better and stop having seizures after a couple of days. It was now December 24, Christmas Eve, and we wanted to take Marie home and thought she was much better but not sure if the doctor would let us take her home yet. The doctor told us that if Marie continued to do okay, she could go home by Christmas. So it was Christmas Eve, as I said, around 4:00 p.m., and the doctor finally came in and told us Marie could go home. We were relieved because we had Joe at home to think about for Christmas. I was afraid there might be a possibility that we would have to stay in the hospital for Christmas as Marie was doing okay seizure-wise and just sleeping.

The day before, Santa had come into Marie's hospital room and she was just sleeping and looked as quiet as the seizures had stopped. I was sad for Marie when the Santa and everyone was singing Christmas carols and passing out toys to the children who were sick in the hospital. I was thinking as they came in and asked if Marie would like a toy. How sad I was for Marie, she doesn't even know it's Christmas and can't enjoy Santa and all the fun. I was feeling sorry for her and myself as I knew she would never know it was Christmas and will never be able to enjoy the holidays. Christmases will come and go and she will never know what she missed. This was her life and we had to learn to deal with these types of events that will come up. I just sat in the dark hospital room and held the stuffed animal that Santa just gave her and cried for Marie and the life she had to live.

Marie's doctor came in the following day to tell us we could take Marie home today. Marie was feeling better and was much more alert. Her seizures seem to have stopped for now.

We gathered Marie's belongings and quickly went home to prepare for Christmas. I had not bought everything for Christmas that I needed, so I quickly ran out to get last minute gifts. We were supposed to be at Steve's mom's house at 6:00 p.m., which didn't happen until around 7:30 to 8:00 p.m. We knew she didn't care and certainly understood. We dragged Marie there and she was so tired. I put on her Christmas dress and dressed Joe in his Christmas outfit. I was trying not to ruin the whole Christmas, more often than not, we had a hospital visit every Christmas it seemed. Marie always seems to wind up in the hospital on or around Christmas for reasons of illness or seizures. We were able to make the best of it. We had to all take turns holding Marie because she was too tired to sit up or stay awake. We only stayed for two hours. Marie just couldn't hold up any longer. So we went home and put her to sleep and wrapped presents for the next few hours to get ready for Joe to have Christmas at home the next day. We have pictures to remember each Christmas and we can tell just by how awful she looks what happened to her each Christmas pretty much. You may wonder how I could possibly drag her around at Christmas to the in-laws. You have to know the years before we had to have everybody in the family move Christmas to our house at the last minute. We had to cancel Christmas sometimes at our house because Marie was just getting out of the hospital. We did have a young son who deserved to have Christmas so we had to celebrate Christmas the best we could for Joe's sake. It was heartbreaking each time we told him on Christmas we could go to his cousins and had to leave early because Marie was not feeling well and seizing. I never knew and still don't know why Marie gets so ill for the holidays. Her nurse said it may be that Marie feels my stress and gets her stressed out and that's how Marie reacts to stress.

I do get really stressed out on holidays because I often have so much to do. I have learned to not get so involved in the holiday and do what I can, but I still have so much to do.

Time to Find a New Doctor

Marie had been displaying these spells that we weren't sure what she was doing. She started about September of 2005 and is still displaying these episodes we called them "lock up" because Marie looked as if she had just froze or her whole body just went rigid. What I mean is every part of her seemed to stop working except her heart. During these episodes, she would go into sweating, staring to the side or ceiling, clenching her fist, her heart rate would escalate, and her eyes would appear to be bulging out. Marie stayed in these episodes for hours and could not eat, sleep, or drink. She also could not focus on anyone or anything and stared out. We felt helpless as we could do nothing but give her Valium and other antidepressant drugs per the doctor's orders to try to calm her down. Marie's neurologist always thought these episodes were panic attacks. After, I insisted that the doctor could take a look at her and told me to just try to get Marie to blow into a bag to get her to relax. I thought that's ridiculous; Marie couldn't blow into a bag in a normal state let alone in this locked up state. We thought these lockups she was having were related to seizures or were actually seizures because they had come after a great deal of medication or Valium was given, but there was no connection there either. She just woke up with them or you could tell she was going into this state.

We even took Marie back to an out-of-state doctor again, and she was really rude to us and told us to go home. There was nothing she could do and didn't have any answers for us. We had asked if there could be damage from what had happened to her when she lost oxygen and the previous hospital lost control of her seizures and how Marie went to intensive care.

We had explained the whole situation, but the only answer this doctor could give us about this disastrous situation we thought horrible was, "That happens all the time here and we can't control that." We left this out-of-state doctor with no answer and no better off after waiting two and a half hours for her. We went home and tried to get Marie's doctor to deal with it.

So we got home and I called the doctor and told her Marie's not getting better with these episodes as it is now seven months of dealing with this "lockup" situation. Anyway, the doctor agreed to give Marie a new medication that works also for seizures. We gave her the dose the doctor prescribed and things seemed to get better and she was not having the episodes as frequent.

April came and Marie was not doing so well on the new drug. She was acting really bizarre. She was behaving like she was on some kind of uppers and screaming out all the time. She seemed as if she was in pain. I called the doctor and told her of Marie's condition, and she said she may be reacting to the medication and was exhibiting side effects that were from the new drug. We then were told to put her on another drug which was similar to the one she was just on.

About a month passed and we started noticing Marie would not eat or drink and was becoming irritable. I called the doctor again and she didn't think it could be the new medication and told us to leave her on it. The doctor told us we could try giving her liquid Valium as she prescribed as a temporary solution. The Valium didn't seem to help as it escalated her mood swings and did not calm her down at all. We had to just deal with this ourselves and we tried to rock Marie for hours in the chair or just hold and comfort her. She would not drink and the nurse was getting worried because we were afraid that she would dehydrate if she wouldn't drink. A day went by and I finally said to take her to the emergency room. I couldn't get fluids into her. The hospital did say when we arrived that Marie was dehydrated and they gave her fluids. We left the hospital after a couple of hours of pumping fluids into Marie. Marie went home and slept, and we kept giving her the prescribed medication her doctor had told us to give. Marie would not drink much, just a little more than she had been which was next to nothing. She would not eat either. As much as the nurse would try, she offered her everything. Marie's favorite foods were not even appealing to her, not even chocolate cake that she loved. We gave her a little bit of fluid each day for about a week. I tried calling the doctor and tried to get her to do something as she was still saying it was not the medication that was just started a month ago. I thought it was the medication making Marie behave the way she was. Marie's nurse also thought it was the medication. She told me she knew of other children who had the same negative side effects that Marie was having. I had to bring Marie in to the hospital again for fear of dehydration. She would hardly drink anything for us now. I had had it with the doctor and began switching to another neurologist in the same practice. I was getting frustrated with Marie's neurologist because she wasn't listening to me. So like I said, I brought Marie back into the hospital for the second time in about two weeks and told them I was afraid Marie was dehydrated again. The doctor in the emergency room was an intern who didn't know Marie. This intern looked at me like I was a nut case and treated me like I belonged in the psych ward. Well, the intern had called Marie's neurologist who insisted there was still nothing wrong with Marie and should not be in the emergency room. The intern, after calling the doctor, reported to me and this is what she said the doctor said, "That mother is not dealing with reality. She can't keep bringing Marie into the hospital to give her fluids and to hydrate Marie!" The intern also informed me that the doctor told her that I dropped her at the end of the month, and she was no longer going to have Marie as a patient. To which I told the intern that is correct due to the fact that this doctor was no longer listening to me when I called her. Granted, I probably was driving her crazy, but I never called unless I had a real problem. We usually tried to deal with Marie ourselves first before going to the doctor. Sometimes, we knew things would pass with Marie. Her conditions came and went at times, but this condition was not stopping. Anyway, the intern, after telling me what Marie's fine doctor said, said he did think Marie was a little dehydrated and did give her fluids and sent us home.

We went home again not sure what to do. Marie was getting worse, not eating or drinking in the last two weeks. She was not eating enough to keep her nutritionally safe. A day went by and Marie was getting worse and screaming out again and shaking every bone in her body and wouldn't sit still. We gave her medication at night and eventually it did get her to sleep after a few hours. I think she just exhausted herself. By the third day, Marie began slowly slipping away. She shook all over and had just kept moving her legs, hands, and feet. She shook her head constantly and did not give us any eye contact. It was as if she was slipping into another world. I didn't sleep at night and said by the morning that I would call her doctor and try again to get her to listen to me and tell her something is very wrong with Marie and to ask for help. I finally got up out of bed, not sleeping all night; it was 5:30 a.m. and I went to check in on Marie and she was awake and was the same and had not slept at all that night. Before, she had been awake and moving and screaming all night. I have a baby monitor which has a video and sound so I can see what she is doing while she is sleeping or when she is having seizures. So I knew she had been up all night because I had been watching her all through the night. I told Steve in the morning before he went to work that I couldn't watch Marie in the state she was in any longer, and to call the doctor when she came in at eight or nine in the morning. Steve was very upset about Marie's condition but didn't know what else we could do but ride it out. Steve had to go to work because we couldn't afford for him to stay home. I put Marie in her chair and she just yelled and moved every bone in her body. She wouldn't eat for me. She looked as though she was going to melt away. She seemed so weak. I was getting scared because I truly thought she was now dying and having hallucinations or had some type of brain damage to cause her to go into some other world that she was in. To look at her, you would think she was on some type of serious drug; she was just out of her mind and stared out and then started to look like she was going to pass out. Marie was only about thirty pounds and losing weight. She was only six years old now.

I had called my mother and told her, "I think Marie is dying. That this was it. This was the final day of Marie's life." I had told my mother that Marie was hallucinating like someone who is dying and drifting off into another world. I knew what someone looked like as they died as I had already witnessed two family members die and Marie looked just as they looked when they were about to die. My mother now was in a complete panic and started crying and told me to call an ambulance. I told my mother I would and I would call her later when she was home from work. Marie's nurse Joan had come in for her shift and was a little early that morning. She looked very worried. Nurse Joan had taken one look at Marie and said to me, "Julie, we have to take her to the hospital. You need to call an ambulance." I just turned to her and started to cry and said. "Do you think she is dying, Joan?" I don't remember what she said except for, "Call the ambulance now, and tell them to shut the sirens off." Why she said shut the sirens off I'm not sure. I did then pick up the phone and called 911. The police showed up first and one of the police officers recognized Marie as he said, "Boy, she has gotten so big since the last time I saw her." I just said, "Yes, is the ambulance on its way?" The police officer was so sweet and said in a calming voice that they are right behind me." We knew most of the cops in town as they had come to our house with the ambulance before many of times. I was hysterical by this time and told the officer, "I think Marie is dying. She has never been like this." The ambulance finally arrived as it seemed like hours before they came. They quickly took her and said her blood pressure was very low and put oxygen on Marie and asked me if she always moves her body so much like this. I went with Marie in the ambulance and

I just watched her thinking this will be the last of Marie coming home. We arrived at the hospital and the doctors looked at her and couldn't understand what was happening to her. The doctor on duty in the emergency room had called Marie's doctor and she came down to talk to us and see Marie. In the meantime, my mother had arrived in the emergency room along with Joan, Marie's nurse; they were both really upset. Poor Joan! The day before, I remember her trying to get Marie to do exercises just to get her to do something to get her mind off things. She had Marie on the floor and was trying to work with her and all of a sudden, she started taking Marie's blood pressure and she couldn't get a heart rate. She got upset and I remember her saying, "I can't get much of a pulse or heart rate, and I just don't hear anything. Oh! I can't lose this one. I just can't." Joan meant, Marie. She couldn't bear losing Marie if she is going to die. Well, then she got a pulse and I remember telling her, "Don't worry, she won't die, Joan. She'll be okay." Not really sure but trying to console her and not get her to upset.

So back we go to the emergency room. Marie's doctor now comes in the room and looks at Marie and says to her nurses that she needs to be put on movement disorder medication because she has a movement disorder. I told the doctor, "She does not have a movement disorder. She just started doing this movement thing where she moves every bone in her body. She never did this before. It has to be the last medication, the new one we just put her on." There were two nurses whom I knew from the neurologist's office with Marie's doctor, and she had an intern with her. I barely noticed the intern but she played a vital role as I will explain later. The doctor told Joan maybe she needed to play with Marie more and keep her more active, put music on to calm Marie. I am not kidding when I tell you this that that was the cause of all of Marie's troubles. We weren't stimulating her enough or not active with her. The nurse does exercises, puts her in her chair, and talks to her and puts her in her stander to watch TV for a half hour. Nurse Joan couldn't do anymore than what she did for Marie. She rocked and held her all the time too. She was great with Marie and truly loved her. I felt sorry for her as the doctor was telling her she wasn't doing enough for Marie. Nurse Joan was so efficient and so competent. She was the wrong nurse to say such terrible things about. After, I told Marie's doctor I thought it was the medication and Marie was not responding. She had never been like this; the doctor still didn't believe a word of what I was saying. The doctor still refused to wean the medicine away to see if she would come back to herself. Steve had showed up after we were put upstairs in a room. The doctor had said she wanted to keep Marie in the hospital to observe her. By putting her in the hospital, they would observe Marie's behavior and thought if they put her on this movement disorder medication, she would be better.

I felt so helpless; I didn't have an ounce of energy left to fight for Marie but knew I had to do something. I talked to Steve into talking to Marie's doctor and see if she would go down on the medication to see if it would show some positive reaction. Steve agreed to talk to her and called her. She said she would talk to him when she was doing rounds the next day.

In the meantime, Marie's nurse went home and my mother and Marie's paternal grandparents also left. I was sitting there in Marie's room so depressed and tired, thinking of what to do. The neurologist who is going to be Marie's new doctor came walking in her hospital room. He had an intern with him who was the same intern who was in the emergency room with Marie's old doctor or present stubborn doctor. Well, anyway, I spoke with her earlier when she stopped in to see how Marie was doing. I forgot I had really talked to her about how that doctor in the emergency wouldn't listen to me and she said I remember it was getting very intense and said she remembered us fighting about Marie's condition. Well, apparently, she went and told (I call him Dr. D., Marie's new neurologist) him that I had thought it was this new drug, clonazepam, was the reason Marie was acting so peculiar. Dr. D. came in and said, "Marie has gotten so big since I last saw her." The doctor knew her, too, but hadn't seen her in a while. All the doctors knew her because she used to go to the hospital so much and whoever was on call for the day or night took care of her. Dr. D. later said to me, "It has been a long road you have been on." To which I just said, "Yes, it has and I'm still on it." He then said the words I never thought I would hear when I asked him to take a shot at what he thought was the matter with Marie. He then said, "Of course, it's the clonazepam. This is exactly what children exhibit when on this medication." I was so relieved; I couldn't believe what he just told me. My battle was over. He then said we would begin weaning Marie off the medication and see how she does but take her off gradually. I knew you can't just stop a medication so he set a plan to wean her off the drug. Marie started doing much better in the next day and became more like the way she was before the medication was started. I did tell Dr. D. that you know Marie is going to be one of your patients. I told him I felt I couldn't stay with her old doctor because she wouldn't listen to me and dismissed everything I said and really just thought I was nuts. Dr. D. probably agreed I was nuts but was to kind to tell me I was.

Marie continued to do well and we went home and didn't start any new medications for a while or at least not right away. I told the doctor I knew he was taking so many new patients as I had heard from parents I knew that had had other doctors in the hospital and now were switching over to Dr. D. I had also said to him that he's going to be a busy doctor because I know a lot of parents of children who are handicapped were all switching to him. He is such a humble doctor that he just said to me, "I'm happy to take care of Marie, I don't mind." He really does love all his kids and takes so much time with each one; every parent I talk to that goes to him loves him. I am so glad I switched doctors as Marie is in much better care. I'm not sure what changed her old doctor's tune about Marie or me for that matter, or why she was so against me all the time. Possibly, I thought maybe, as she often told me, the doctors at the other hospital never kept her informed of Marie's care when we had to switch hospitals and doctors because the one locally ran out of options. The second hospital sent us back to the first and original children's hospital because the doctor there said Marie's seizures were under control, and he didn't know anything about her "lock up" condition. The old hospital could look into it and her new doctor was doing research on conditions that Marie might have. So I'm not sure what went wrong with Marie's old doctor, but she had Marie since her first seizure when Marie was seven months old. I felt sorry to lose her but felt I didn't have any choice. I needed someone who was going to listen to me and take care of Marie.

I really do drive doctors crazy. Sometimes, I might think I know more than the doctors, but I am learning to shut up when I don't. I will still fight them if I truly believe I know something is very wrong with Marie and they are just not looking at the whole picture. I make them look and they know now I'm not going away until I get an answer. I used to not be so aggressive and just be so shy and easy going. Now I do have to get my Irish up now and again with people when it comes to both my children. Joe doesn't require any appointment with doctors as he is always healthy. The doctors always ask when they see me how Joe is. They probably wonder if Joe gets any attention with Marie taking so much of us. Joe does get his share of attention. We make sure of it. He is really a bit spoiled because we overdo with him because of Marie.

So this was another one of Marie's terrible traumatic times in her life and she made it through again. Thank goodness. We get stronger each time, I think.

On May 21, 2005, we celebrated Marie's sixth birthday. We had a beautiful princess cake made at the bakery for her. Marie enjoyed her chocolate cake and ate every bite of her piece. It is always a challenge to find birthday gifts for Marie; we usually try to get her musical toys because she really enjoys listening to music and also colorful children's movies. She seems to enjoy seeing everyone and enjoyed her big day.

The end of May and June went well and Marie was finishing her year of kindergarten. I loved her teacher and her teacher really seems to like having Marie in her class. She always told me she did. I liked her kindergarten teacher so much I requested Joe to have her the following year for he was going to kindergarten the next fall.

Marie went on in June to a summer camp they have in our town for special education children. Marie didn't attend summer camp to many days because the day started at 9:00 a.m. and she just couldn't wake up that early. She was used to going to school at 11:00 a.m. in the school year. We kept her at home and kept her busy enough during the days.

Big Changes Had
to Come Ahead

In July, Marie was still doing well and her seizures had developed into a new phase. She was having what we called knockout seizures. Marie would all of a sudden just collapse out of nowhere and have a seizure. Marie had these knockout seizures when she was awake in the middle of the day or in the early night; it didn't matter what time. She would just fall flat where she was sitting or standing. We always had to be ready for these seizures to happen. The physical therapist who works with Marie at home made her a cushion that we could put on her chair, table, and stander in case she has a knockout seizure. Thank goodness, the physical therapist had thought of this because we were just using towels to pad the shelves, but sometimes would forget, and Marie was not protected and would hit her head on whatever she landed on. The poor girl had a few bangs and bruises by the time her physical therapist came up with the padding that we could transfer to any table she had in front of her so she would not keep hurting herself when having a knockout seizure. These seizures didn't last long; a minute or two and she was over it. Marie would become tired after having a knockout seizure and needed to lie down.

We learned to just be aware that Marie could have a seizure at any time now and fall right down. It was scary when you saw her have a knockout seizure. When I called the doctor's office, Marie's neurologist explained the seizures she was having. The nurse told me that these seizures, what we called knockout seizures was just that. The doctor's nurse said that is what they call them because they are just that. When the person is having this seizure, they do just go right down and look like they are knocked out. The doctor said to increase one of her seizure meds and said to give it time to activate into her brain. So we did.

We went to my mother's cottage at the beach and were going to stay for a week. Marie's nurse was going to travel back and forth each day to be with Marie to watch her at the beach house. I thought it was great. We could go to the beach and I could spend time with my son Joe and time with my mother and our family, too.

Nurse Joan came each day and brought her daughter and grandson one day. They enjoyed the beach, but the nurse's grandson seemed to be a little jealous of Marie and didn't like his grandmother paying attention to someone besides him. We were having a great time and my friends had come down and I enjoyed spending time with them while Marie's nurse took care of her so I could go to the beach. Marie did have quite the knockout seizure though and I remember the nurse yelling for me to come quickly and get Marie out of the stander as she just collapsed. I did get Marie out of her stander and held her and then gave her to the nurse. Joan held her for a while and then I put her down for a nap in the air-conditioned room. We always had to have Marie in air-conditioning in the summer as the heat induced a seizure, too. Marie was fine and slept most of the day but was up later on. We took her for a walk at the beach and she was much better.

The rest of the week went by fast; our vacation came to an end. We really had a good week, although Marie had one more knockout seizure on the last day of our vacation. We had to leave early to get her home to rest or we would have to stay another night. Marie had a tendency to sleep for long periods of time from seizures and even into the next day.

We arrived back home after a nice week. Nothing exciting happened. We had to get back to living without going to the beach each day, but we would go back down on the weekends.

All was fine the following Monday after we just came back from our vacation at the beach. It was August 1 now and Nurse Joan was due any minute now as I heard the phone ring. I picked it up upstairs and it was a woman from the nursing agency. I don't even remember her name. What she told me next was a complete shock. She told me they would have to find us another nurse because our nurse Joan gave her two weeks' notice and would be leaving us in two weeks. I had to have her repeat what she said because I told her nurse Joan never mentioned this to me. I was with her all last week at the beach. I did notice that nurse Joan had called the nursing agency's office once or twice the week before and was having a problem with them because they wouldn't pay for her vacation; she had taken a couple of weeks in May.

I hung up the phone and heard Joan come in and thought I will clear this big mistake up. I went downstairs and went to her and said, "Joan I just received a call from the agency and they said you were leaving us?" She just stared at me and then said, "I can't believe they called. I told them not to. I wanted to tell you myself." To which I said, "So it's true you're leaving?" She said, "Julie, I'm sorry, but I have to. The agency doesn't give me any benefits as far as insurance or vacation. The agency was supposed to pay me for vacation but never did." She said the vacation wasn't a big deal, but she needed health insurance and she had found a real good job with health insurance that was an administrative position. Nurse Joan was an older lady and I knew she couldn't work for Marie forever, and the agency doesn't give their nurses health benefits. I was heartbroken because it took us so long to find a good nurse, and I knew I would have to go down that road again and start all over. It was so difficult for a nurse to get to know Marie and all her little quirks. Joan did say she wanted to be in Marie's life and never wants to be out of her life and would like to still watch her on weekends when I needed her.

I just had to accept the fact that Marie's nurse was leaving after almost two years of being with her. I did get up the nerve to start looking and the agency said they would look too. The two weeks went by quickly and Marie's nurse left and I was so sorry to see her go when she finally did and said good-bye. It was easier because we knew she would be still a part of our life and Marie's and would work on weekends.

The agency called the following week and sent a new nurse out for us to see if she would be a good match for Marie. The new nurse showed up and she was young and very pretty. I thought she was great right off the bat; she was happy, bright, and sweet as could be and full of life. I knew she was going to be great as I showed her everything, and she acted like she knew how to do all we needed her to do for Marie right from the first day. Joe our son loved her as she was so nice to him and gave him so much attention, too. The new nurse was great and we had our nightmare of finding a nurse over. She said she would love to take care of Marie and started immediately. I was so relieved and relaxed with her. She was so competent and carried Marie around the house on her hip like Marie was a two-year-old baby.

It was mid-August when this new nurse had started. Her name was Jill. We had decided that she was going to go to first grade with Marie and stay with her all day at school. The other nurses never did but Marie's seizures were so difficult to predict that we thought it was best for Marie and the school staff to have the nurse go to school with her.

I did have another battle ahead of me as far as the nurse going to school with Marie. The town I live in had to deny paying for Marie to have a nurse go to school with her in order for Marie's state insurance to pick up payment. This denial of payment was of course another fight I had to go through to get help for Marie. Everything always seems to be a fight to have the simplest need met for Marie in order for Marie to have access to functions in society with her special needs. This was a battle I had to go through, but in the end, I did succeed in getting the nurse to go to school with Marie.

The school year began and Marie had another nice teacher and I thought things would be great this year for her with the pieces all in place. Things were normal at home and things were good at school.

Getting Marie to Gain Weight

The fall went well and Marie was in school and doing well, not making any miracles happen but she was okay. Marie was six and Joseph was five, and both in school full time. I went to work more hours since I could now that they were not in need of me to care for them as much during the day.

Marie needed to get a feeding tube put in as she was not gaining enough weight and still at six years old was very tall but only weighed 31 lb. and fluctuated from 29 lb. to 31 lb. quite a bit at times. We had fought so hard not to put a feeding tube in, but Marie was having difficulty chewing her food and choking on her food. She no longer wanted to take her medicine no matter how we disguised it. We put it in everything to have her swallow it, but she refused most of the time. We had to put the feeding tube in around October.

We made all the arrangements with the hospital for the day of surgery for Marie to get the feeding tube inserted. I knew it was a step in the right direction but also knew it was a setback for Marie because I thought this was a function that she would never have a problem with. She used to eat so well and enjoyed food and her bottles. We finally got her to take a different kind of cup and get rid of her bottles, although she fought us every step of the way. I thought she would never get off the bottles. She did and at least this goal had been achieved. *Yea*!

Marie had the feeding tube put in and we had to let her stay in the hospital overnight. We didn't know this but we had to learn how to hook her up to a feeding pump at night to have nutrition being put in her even through the night and give her this special formula. The whole feeding thing was new to us and no one ever explained to us that we needed to have special formulas or that we needed a pump that had to be run all night.

The nurses had to get a special technician to come in from a medical equipment company to show us how to operate the feeding tube pump. The person from the medical equipment company came to the hospital and brought us the feeding pump and all the parts that goes with it. This guy from the company refused to show us how to use it saying it wasn't his job to show us. The nurse at the hospital said that it was and he needed to show us. After a long dispute between the two, the employees just simply skimmed on instructing us on what we needed to do. The nurse did show us when she was able to get a free minute and I mean minute. She didn't have the time either. We went home the following day after Marie had the feeding tube put in and still had no clue how to use the machine. Steve had a little bit of an idea, but I was in no way going to know how.

So we left and I called the nursing agency to see if they could tell us how the feeding machine should be used. The hospital had told us to call the agency and they would know the feeding requirements and maintenance of the machine. They sent a nurse out the next day. The nurse arrived on Sunday morning about 7:30 a.m. Why she had to come that early I don't know, but she did show us how to use the feeding pump/machine.

We tried the feeding pump for Marie that Sunday night and the damn thing was going off every hour; it just didn't stop. Steve thought each time he hooked it up to the correct time, but it still went off each hour. It went on like this for the first few nights, and eventually, we got better at setting the feeding pump. I say we but I never did. Steve always hooked it up. I just poured the formula in the bag and acted like I was doing it all. Steve became great with setting up the feeding pump as I became less knowledgeable of the whole thing altogether. I just didn't want to figure it out. I think it was such a pain in my neck. I must have figured, Steve can do this. I don't need to learn. It can be his job and he did it. I never really did much with her feeding pump and we eventually didn't need it because we gave her formula with her meals now, too, in her bottle.

As the months went on, Marie gained weight and medicine was no longer a problem. We just put all her medicine through the feeding tube. People told me the feeding tube would make our life easier too, but I never wanted to believe it or want it to make my life easier. I just wanted Marie to eat. In the end, it was a blessing to have the feeding tube put in and I realized it.

I now told moms who were going through this weight gaining problem with their child, how I fought the feeding tube, and in the end, I don't know what we would have done without it.

Marie was doing well as the time went on and we were getting adjusted to the feedings. She now gained eight pounds in the first five months. However, Marie would cry in pain after each feeding. We found out the crying every time after feeding her was gas pains and that the formula didn't agree with her—she was allergic to the formula. We needed to switch formulas. One of her doctors kept telling me to give her more formula, she will get used to it. I kept calling him and telling him something was wrong and that she cries after I feed her. I finally made an appointment with a different doctor because Marie's doctor couldn't see her right away. The doctor I saw noticed right away after I gave her the milk in the office how uncomfortable she became and said it was the formula making her so ill and upset her stomach and giving her pain. So he switched formulas and Marie has been fine since then.

Always a battle, nothing ever comes easy with Marie. There seems to always be a catch to a good thing when it comes to Marie. There is always a curveball thrown her way and you need to watch out for her always. So the formula was the problem, but we had to go through hell again to figure it out.

After the formula problem was solved, things went well for the next few months. Marie continues to gain weight and be happy.

Okay with Little Marie, but Grandma Marie Not So Good

My mother, Grandma Marie, as my children called her, was not feeling very well. My mother was getting sick and had a cough. We figured it was just a cold and she would feel better in a few days. It was now February of 2006. My mom's birthday was in February and we had dinner and a family party for her. She looked tired but had a great time. I had noticed at my son's birthday party, at the end of January, that my mother looked thinner and was losing weight. My mother always tried to lose weight but never could until my father passed away and then her weight went down a great deal. My mother was losing a lot of weight and when I looked at her and asked her why, she said she didn't know. She just wasn't hungry for what she used to eat. Anyway, she developed a cough in February and we brought her to her doctor. He said she had bronchitis and to give her a prescription medicine and she will feel better.

A month went by but my mother still had a cough and wasn't feeling too well. We brought her back to the doctor and he said it was still bronchitis and gave her more medicine. My mother took the medicine and I remember going to the pharmacy to fill the prescription. My mother was too weak to get out of the car but insisted she go in to get the prescription filled. So I went in with her afraid she would fall. My mother was a heavyset woman and strong, but I knew she was getting thinner and weaker by the day.

Another month went by and it was March. My entire family was supposed to go to the St. Patrick's Day parade, which was sort of a tradition. We went every year and then everyone came back to my house and we celebrated. On the day we were to go to the parade, my younger sister Joan called me, my mother was staying with her at her house to tell me they couldn't go and she was not sure what was wrong with our mother but she was very ill. I told my sister to bring her to the hospital and have her checked out or I would take her. We were going back and forth on the phone and trying to decide what to do with my mother. My mother insisted she did not want to go to the hospital and so they stayed home. I did too, but I had my friends and family members coming to my house for the St. Patrick's Day party. I wasn't sure what to do and everyone told me to have the party, positive my mother would be okay. So I did have the party and talked to my sister Joan on the phone. Joan lived about a half hour to forty-five minutes away from me. We had the party and I did worry about my mother throughout the day, but I couldn't help her today. The following day, my mother continued to get worse and started spitting up blood. We knew there was something very wrong with her, but her doctor insisted all the time it was just bronchitis and she would be okay.

On Monday morning, I took her to the emergency room as my mother was even weaker and so sick she couldn't function. We waited in the emergency room for six hours before they even called my mother in. I had to go home to check on my family and my older sister Mary came to stay at the hospital while my mother waited for a doctor to examine her. Mary was finally called in and where my mother had been given a room. The doctor who examined my mother told Mary that her mother is very sick, and they have to run more tests and that she would be admitted to the hospital.

A couple of hours more went by and my sister Mary was still with my mother when I went back to the hospital. The doctor had come back and told my sister, after running the tests, that my mother had lung cancer and was very sick from it. He said she had stage two cancer and needed to see an oncologist right away.

My sister told the doctor that we had brought my mother to her doctor twice and he said she had bronchitis. The doctor just said, "I'm sorry you were told wrong. Your mother has cancer." My sister was in shock and then called all of our family to inform everyone of what was wrong with my mother. We knew we had to tell my mother. We had decided to tell her the next day gradually to not break her spirit. She was shocked when she had found out she had cancer. My mother, I think, knew there was something seriously wrong with her but certainly didn't think it was cancer. My mother was always healthy and was still young, we thought. She was only seventy-four years old. My brothers and sisters all came to see my mother the next day in the hospital. My mother's doctor—the one who kept saying she had bronchitis—came to see my mother, and my older brother and I were sitting there with her. My older brother Larry asked the doctor, "How could you not see this? Why did you keep diagnosing my mother with bronchitis and said her x-rays just showed fluid on her lungs and might be pneumonia." The doctor didn't have any kind of explanation and not any real remorse.

The doctor just said he had been practicing many years and these things happen. There was no point in arguing with the doctor and my brother didn't pursue a further explanation from the doctor because he wasn't getting anywhere with him anyway. I can remember telling my brother he is just covering himself (the doctor) and forget it. Arguing with him wasn't going to get rid of my mother's cancer. My mother was also in the room, and she didn't like people to get upset. She practically made that a rule in her life always pleasing everyone else, not herself. We didn't want to upset my mother or add any more stress to her, so we had to move on to what was the next plan of action to take—to cure my mother's lung cancer.

The oncologist, who was now her doctor for her cancer, started her on chemotherapy the following week. My brothers and sisters took turns taking my mother to chemotherapy in the weeks that followed. My mother lived with me during the week and on the weekends went to my younger sister Joan's house. We made my mother's living arrangements this way because I lived fifteen minutes away from the hospital where she had chemotherapy since my mother had treatments during the week and took breaks from it on the weekends. My brother, sister, and my mother's cousin and her daughter went to the oncologist with my mother to talk about her prognosis. The daughter of my mom's cousin went to the appointments with her because she was an intern and could help us to have a better understanding of what the doctors were telling us. Although the oncologist was very kind and said he would do everything he could to help my mother, he wasn't sure— or what he really said was he couldn't cure her since her cancer was so far along.

After hearing the news that the oncologist couldn't say he could cure my mother, we were still hopeful that the chemotherapy treatments would prolong her life. We tried to keep my mother positive as she was a very positive person any way and very optimistic. We kept taking my mother to chemotherapy and it made her so sick; her hair was beginning to fall out right away. She became so weak and tired after treatments and it was getting hard for her to function and do her daily living activities. By the second month, we had to give her breathing treatments and let her rest most of the time. My mother enjoyed being at each one of my brother's and sister's house while she was ill. She enjoyed the grandchildren and they kept her entertained always when she was able to sit and talk to them. At my house, it was always kind of crazy as there was always something going on with Marie's condition, and Joe loved reading and going in and talking to his grandmother. I had three cats who always managed to end up sleeping next to my mother or even sometimes I caught them in the morning curled up on her top. I have two big dogs that always managed to go and sneak up on my mom and kiss her or just wanted her to pet them. My mother always liked having the animals in my house around her though. I had to throw them out of her room, which was my living room and my mom would say, "Leave them, they're okay. They don't bother me. I like the cats and dogs near me." I sometimes would leave her with one dog or cat, and she fell asleep petting one of them. Joe was so disappointed when his grandma Marie would go to my other sister's house as he loved having her there to play with. She made him laugh. My sister Joan's kids loved having their grandma at their house and they loved entertaining her, too. My mother still was able to go to church with my sister and tried to join some groups in her town. My mother was a very active member in the community where she lived and was a member of a few charitable groups. I think one of the most difficult things my mother had to endure was giving up her membership to the groups she belonged to because of her cancer.

The next two months, my mother became sicker and sicker between the chemotherapy and the cancer; she was unable to walk and had to use a walker. My mother couldn't eat because of chemotherapy and drinking was difficult, too. In August, we had to take her to the hospital as she was having difficulty breathing. The hospital put her on oxygen and let her go back home. I had to meet my sister halfway between her house and mine in the middle of the night because my sister was going to keep Mom at her house because I had to work the next day.

My mother wanted to go to the beach house and stay there for the rest of the summer. My brother and his family were there to stay with her and could take care of her so she could go.

My mother ended up in the hospital for a few days to get her oxygen level back up. I took her because she couldn't breathe again. The hospital said she had to go to a convalescent home for awhile just so she could get her strength back. We took her to a convalescent home that we knew of and the hospital arranged it. When we arrived, it was hard to adjust to this arrangement because it seemed so depressing to leave my mother there. My older sister was so upset that when we arrived, my sister Mary said to me, "I only want my Mom to stay here for one week. That's it and then she's out of here." To which I said, "Don't worry, it will only be a week and then she can leave here. We are not leaving her to live here." My mother was her usual optimistic self and it was really her idea to go there and told us she was just going there to get stronger and learn to walk again.

I had to agree with my mother and fought with her to come to my house, but I knew she couldn't walk and I was having a hard time lifting her when I did at my house, and my sister had difficult time lifting my mother also at her home. We knew we had to put her in a place that had therapist to help her get stronger.

Between Marie, Grandma Marie, Joe and having to work, life was getting challenging to keep up the pace. All of us were pretty exhausted by then and needed a new plan. We wouldn't have it any other way to take care of our mother and to do the very most and everything we could to help her. My mother was there for everyone of her six children and her eleven grandchildren. She always gave us her all and a hundred percent of herself when we needed her. It was the only way we knew to do everything possible to take care of her.

The week went by in the convalescent home and we saw my mother getting stronger every day and eating better. She even looked better and was able to walk up and down the halls each day. By the end of the week, my older sister Mary went to pick up my mother and take her home from the convalescent home. Mary arrived in my driveway and could barely get out of the car and get my mother out before she started to cry. When I asked her what was the matter, she managed to get out the words and tell me. Mary said when she picked up my mother, the director of the convalescent home told her, "You can't bring your mother back here if she becomes weak. Your mother is too ill to be in this type of convalescent home." I couldn't believe she said that either since we thought my mother was doing better now. We kept this information in mind but had to keep going with the next plan, which was to get my mother to the beach house where she wanted to be.

In two days, my mother left for the beach house and was going to live there for the rest of the summer and into September. My mother loved it at the beach. She had been going down there to her beach house all her life. Her house was the third or fourth house back in the 1930s—the only houses on the beach. My mom's house was a big old house on the waterfront. So she went and loved staying with my brother and his wife and the four children, and my mother was happy.

After being at the beach for a week, my mother had to come back to the oncologist to talk again about what to do with treatment. My brothers and sisters and my mother's cousin and her daughter all went to talk to the oncologist. When we went in to talk to the doctor, he was not very optimistic. He said there was nothing more he could do for my mother. The cancer was no longer treatable. He said also that he was not going to prescribe any more medications as he thought all was done. My mother's cousin who was a doctor asked him to prescribe antidepressants, but he refused saying he didn't think my mother needed them as she seemed psychologically okay with her illness. He probably thought we needed them more than my mother. My older brother began to argue with him, telling him he didn't think the doctor was doing enough, and giving up to early in this stage of her illness. The oncologist refused to do anything more and told us to let my mother die peacefully and for us to accept it.

Well, I thought he was being a jerk, this oncologist, and had never indicated anything before this that nothing could be done. He had refused to help her when I called to notify him about my mother's legs being so swollen and he refused to put her on a diuretic, he said she didn't need it. This oncologist was not one of my favorite doctors anyway, so I didn't give him much credit. At the beginning of my mother's illness, he was not very nice and seemed a little arrogant. Of course, we didn't like him now because he wasn't telling us what we wanted to know, and that being that our mother was cured, anything short of that, we were not going to listen.

After leaving the oncologist's office my family members and I began looking for a new doctor, one who could help my mother. I don't think we were looking for a cure or maybe we were but we had to help my mother.

It was the beginning of September when we met with a new doctor at a new hospital with a great reputation for cancer care. We met with the doctor, an oncologist, who was very young and as my mother said, "Very good-looking." He was bright and pleasant. We liked everything about him. He told us he could help my mother although he did tell us right from the start he couldn't cure her cancer. He told us with chemotherapy and radiation, my mother may have more time to live, maybe a year to a year and a half. We were pleased and he said that my mother would have to start radiation right away and they had a new therapy that wouldn't make her so sick.

By the following week, I took my mother to the new hospital where she would start treatment. My brother's wife was there to see my mother and stayed with her during her treatment. The nurses got my mother started on her treatment and my sister-in-law was going to stay with my mother. I left the hospital and was going back to get my mother after she was finished. I had to get Joe from school so I hurried home and checked on Marie and went to get Joe and then back to get my mother.

My mother seemed upbeat and a little more relaxed. She was relieved now that she had hoped again too that this new treatment would buy her time. For the next three weeks, we kept taking my mother to treatments at the cancer center. My mother started getting weak again and sick all the time from the treatments. Her oncologist kept saying to go on with the treatments as long as she could. We took my mother back to the beach house as often as she wanted to and felt up to it. It was getting cold now as it was September and fall was setting in. The kids all went back to school and I had to go back to work.

Through my entire mother's illness, Marie was doing well and didn't need to go into the hospital. She had a nasal sinus infection and colds through the last few months but was doing well. We always had to worry about the kids getting my mother sick as she didn't need any more problems to add to her already devastating illness. We had to keep whoever children were sick away from my mother, so she wouldn't catch anything they had or carried.

We did manage to pick up my mother and one of us would take her to her treatments and work out a schedule so that my mother was always taken care of. My mother hated being a burden because as she always put it, she was so independent. My mother was the most selfless person I know and always put everyone's needs before her own. She was so easy to take care of and really never complained unless she was in real pain.

Marie at three weeks old with Dad

Grandpa, Grandma, and Marie at Baptism, Aug. 1999

Marie with Mom and Grandma at beach house, Aug. 1999

Marie at beach house, Aug. 1999

Marie at Attawan Beach, one year old

Marie's first birthday with Mom and Dad

Marie after a bath, six months

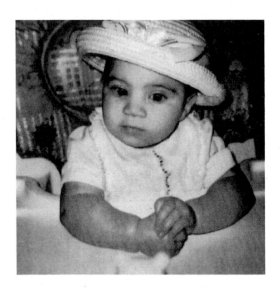

Marie in Easter outfit, fourteen months

Marie, two and a half years old

Marie Feb. 2001, twenty–one months

Marie, two years; and Joseph, four months

Marie and Joe, Xmas Dec. 2002

Marie at Easter 2005, six years old

Marie, two and a half years; and Joe, eleven months. Xmas 2001

Marie, two and a half years; and Joe,
ten months, with Mom, Oct. 2002

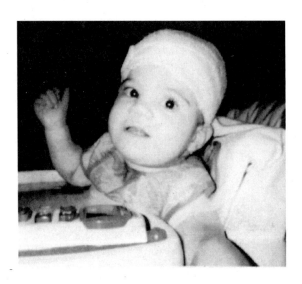

Marie during EEG with gauze around
head to keep electrodes in place

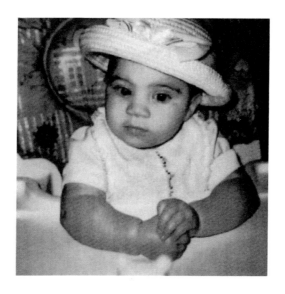

Marie in Easter outfit, April 2002, age fourteen months

Marie, 2 years; and Joseph, ten months. Dec. 2001

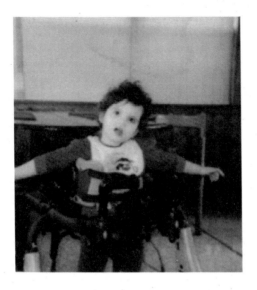

Marie in walker, May 2002, learning to walk

Marie with her Dad, ten months

Marie on Halloween, three years

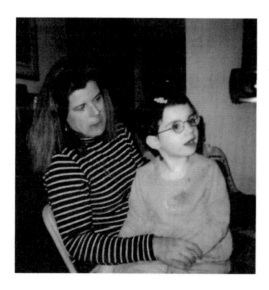

Marie, three years, and Mom, Nov. 2002

Marie and Grandma after brain surgery, May 2002

Marie and Mom, third birthday right after brain surgery

Marie on school bus, four years old

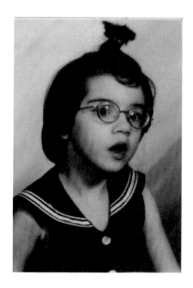

Marie, kindergarten, five years old

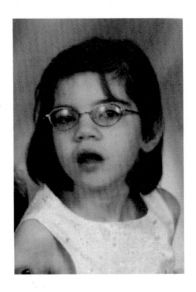

Marie, six years old, first grade

Marie, seven years old, second grade

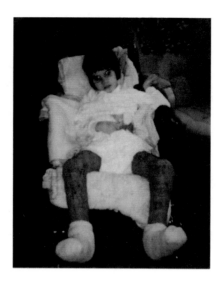

Marie's full-body cast for hip correction,
eight years old, first cast

Dad, Mom, Marie, and Joe, Disney World, Feb. 2008

Marie, Mom, Grandma, Joe, Dad,
and Grandpa at Give Kids the World

Marie and Dad in pool at Give Kids the World

Marie rides a horse in Feb, Give Kids the World, eight years old

Marie with Santa, family, Sam and Malley

Marie and Joe at Marie's First Communion

Marie meets Minnie Mouse at Disney World

Marie with Grandpa on her tenth birthday

For Grandma Marie

In the beginning of October, my mother started getting even weaker each day. We brought her to the hospital and they admitted her due to excessive bleeding internally. The doctors found where she had been bleeding and cauterized it. My mother came out of the surgery and was doing well. She went home again and was feeling okay. Another two weeks went by and she started feeling ill and weak, so they put her back in the hospital and said the bleeding had started again and they would have to stop it again.

The oncologist did say they would try to get her bleeding to stop but were unsure it would work. So they went in again and stopped the bleeding. After a week, my mother went home. My mother went back to almost normal. She was still very sick and couldn't eat. We then were told by the doctors we would have to think about getting respite care for her. My sister had called me and said my mother wasn't feeling well and needed to go to the hospital.

I took my mother to the hospital with Joe. The hospital admitted her and was looking into what could be wrong. It was November 18, 2005, when my mother went into the hospital. The doctor said they needed to find the bleeding again and stop it; it was making her so weak. They went in the day after and stopped the bleeding and gave her a blood transfusion. They put my mother in intensive care to watch her. On the Sunday after the surgery, two days later, I went to see my mother in intensive care and she was doing well. She was alert and she looked better than she had in nine months. She was back to herself and stronger than ever. I did not get to see her in a couple of days prior to this Sunday because Steve's grandmother passed away. My mother was able to get on the phone and call my mother-in-law and talk to her and send her condolences for her mother's passing. She spoke to my mother-in-law for a little while but could only stay on the phone for a short time. She was still weak. I left my mother shortly after and my sister stayed with her when I left and my brothers were coming. I told my mother I would be back in a day or two as I had to go to Steve's grandmother's wake and funeral in the next two days.

The next day, I talked to my mother on the phone and she was alert and doing well. They were going to move her out of intensive care and put her in a regular room.

I came back on Wednesday to see my mother and brought Joe with me to see his grandmother Marie. Joe played on her bed and drew in a book and watched TV. I noticed my mother was not too clear and her memory was starting to fail. She wasn't making sense; she was not following what I was saying to her at all. The hospital wanted to get some tube down her throat but she wouldn't let them. She said it bothered her too much. My mother never did let them put the tube down her throat which wasn't like her. I remember watching Oprah and my mother just stared at the TV and didn't talk. It was like she was in another world. I thought maybe she was tired and needed to rest so I told her I'll be back tomorrow. My sister and brother and his wife came. My brothers John and Bob called her while I was there and she wasn't making sense with them either. I left and my sister-in-law came downstairs with me and I told her I thought something was wrong with my mother; she didn't make sense. My sister-in-law assured me that my mother was just tired. I left and called her when I got home and called my sister and said my mother didn't seem right. The next day was Thanksgiving and I was going early to see my mother and spend some time with her.

The next morning, I went to get ready to leave and my answering machine was going off and my mother was on it. I couldn't tell what she was saying but yelling at me. She told me she needed me at the hospital and if I could hurry and get there. This wasn't like her to beg for me to come see her. She never demanded any attention, but this time she was telling me to come to the hospital and how she needed me there.

When I arrived, I saw my mother sitting in the chair talking to a nurse and talking crazy. She introduced me to the nurse and kept talking and making no sense. I called the nurse outside and asked her if she thought my mother was losing her mind. The nurse didn't know my mother and said so but also said she thought she was okay. After talking to my mother, she made no sense and couldn't place anything in her mind. I left the room and went to find a phone and called my sisters and told them that I thought they needed to come to the hospital that our mother was losing her mind and I thought she was dying. I know how you can lose your mind as I said I saw two family members one being my dad lose his mind just before he died.

My younger sister was on her way to see our mother anyway so she said she will figure things out when she got there. My sister came and she talked with her and thought she was okay; not great but not as bad as I thought she was.

141

I told Steve to take the kids to my mother-in-law's house as they were going there for Thanksgiving dinner. I wanted Joe not to miss Thanksgiving or Steve because it was their holiday, too. I stayed at the hospital for a while and left knowing my sister was going to stay with my mother for the rest of the day. I left the hospital and went to my mother-in-law's house for a while to be with them again. I know Joe would have been disappointed if I didn't go at all to celebrate Thanksgiving. I wasn't in the mood to go but had to. So I said good-bye to my mother and told her I would be back later or in the morning.

Later, when I came home from Thanksgiving at my in-laws, I called my sister and said I was really worried about Mom. We both agreed we would go first thing in the morning. I didn't sleep at all that night. I could not stop thinking about my mother. Friday morning, I went to see my mother and she was much worse and not making any sense. I stayed for a while that day and my mother kept sleeping. I finally left her sleeping and kissed her and told her I'll be back later. My sister was going to see her and said she slept most of the time she was there, too. I didn't go back that night. I thought my mother could use the rest so I stayed home.

I didn't sleep at all; I was worried about my mother. At about 6:00 a.m., Saturday, November 26, 2005, I heard the phone ring and told my husband to quickly pick it up. Steve picked up the phone and my sister Joan had called and said the hospital just called her and my mother died. I was in shock and had to hear my sister tell us again. I couldn't believe she was gone. I went to the hospital with my brother to see her one more time. I suppose I needed to see that she really died.

I went with my brother, John, and it was, to say the least, heart wrenching to see my mother still there and lifeless. I didn't know how I was going to go on without her. We had a priest come and my brothers and sisters came to say prayers over her, and we knew she had a place in heaven.

We went home and my brothers and sisters and I began making her funeral arrangements. It was the most difficult thing I ever had to do. We got through the next few days and had my mother's wake and funeral. The priest went to school with my mother and knew her well and spoke about all the great charitable contributions she made to the world.

I need to just tell you briefly, what a kind, caring, considerate, fun, loving, generous women my mother was. She gave anyone who needed it a bed to stay in at our home if they were in any kind of trouble. She brought African American children about six to eight kids to her beach house for the week to give them a place to enjoy just to let them have some enjoyment for a week. My mother took so much verbal abuse from people in her beach association for bringing the African American kids to the beach, but she didn't care she always said, I don't care what they think. She wanted to show others to be kind, and that they had a right to be there, too. My father had many surprises when he came home from work as my mother would tell him somebody needed help and he would say, "Marie, what poor soul have you found now to stay and live with us." My mother was always doing well for people. She sought out people who needed help and they knew who to go to. I could go on and on about all the acts of kindness she did but, it would take up pages and pages. She was funny and Joe my son always laughs when he thinks of Grandma Marie. He laughs about how she taught him to eat backwards, to eat dessert first. She would often say at dinner to all the kids, "Hey, you wanna eat backwards?" Of course, the kids would say, "Yeah! Grandma let's do that." I would ask my mother when I was younger, "Why do you do all these things for people?" My mother would respond, "I want to make the world a better place for them, and I want people to remember me that way." I said at the end of her eulogy, "Mom, you did make the world a better place, and everyone will remember you for that and for all you did."

Looking Ahead

The next couple of months went by uneventfully. Our family was trying to get adjusted to life without Steve's grandmother and my mother. Christmas came and went and it was a difficult Christmas being without my mother and Steve's grandma, but we had to find a way to get through it for all the kids in the family. They were all young enough to love Christmas and the presents they got spoiled with. We did miss both of them very much this year.

The next two months went by and I decided I wanted to try one last time to see if Marie could be diagnosed with some syndrome or answers to what was wrong with her. Marie was seven years old now and we thought being older, we could maybe get an answer to her problem. The very least we wanted to find out was what we called "lock up" that Marie had. We wanted to know what that was all about or what caused her to go into this state of mind she goes into. So I called my cousin who was doing her internship at a hospital out of state and she gave me a name of a neurologist. The next day, I called the neurologist and I was given an appointment by her receptionist for the following month.

The month went by quickly and we were going to see the new neurologist who was in a children's hospital out of state. We had to get Marie up early that morning and she was really sleepy, but we got her to the appointment. The doctor looked her over and did a thorough check on her and Marie just happens to be in "lock up" that day so the doctor could see what we were talking about. Marie was out of it and just stared out and didn't respond to the doctor at all. The doctor said she didn't know what this was but she could run tests and she had hoped to get some answers through blood work. We went to another department in the hospital to get the blood work done on Marie as the doctor ordered. The new neurologist was very nice and compassionate and really cared about Marie's well-being. She said she would see us again in another three months to follow up with us, and we made the appointment to see her in three months.

When we returned home, Marie went about the next few weeks doing her normal routine and going to school with her nurse and having fun. About a month after we saw the new neurologist, she had called to tell us she didn't have any answers to the blood work, but would like to see us to talk about Marie.

I had called the doctor that Marie saw here, her neurologist, and asked him if there was anything he knew to stop Marie's lockup condition. He said we could try a new medication and see if that could calm her episodes down a bit. We agreed to give her this new medication and give it a try. After a couple of weeks went by, Marie's episodes of lock up seemed to get further apart in time as they were happening less frequently.

Another Crisis with Marie

It was now the end of April. The spring is finally here and Marie is doing okay on her new medication. We noticed Marie not wanting to eat and not herself. She was becoming more lethargic each day and slipping in her daily functions. Marie was still her alert self but acting as if she was getting ill, like with a flu or some type of stomach virus. One day, she started throwing up and we just felt she was getting a stomach virus so we just treated her with the usual things you do when a child is sick to their stomach and gave her fluids and rest.

When starting a new medication, I am always watching for any side effects, but did not see any with the new drug, Baclofen. She had been on Baclofen now for about a month and it seems to be helping with her lock up condition, and she was having a fewer episodes.

Marie was constantly throwing up after three days of being sick. We called the pediatrician, and he had said there is a lot of that going around and to give her some time to feel better. The doctor had said it could be a week to ten days this virus may last. Day 4 started and Marie was throwing up all the time, and we were not able to do anything to help her. Marie's nurse Jill was telling me I should take her to the doctor's office. I had told her give it another day and see if she gets better. The doctor had already told me to give the virus a week to ten days to disappear.

After a day went by, I couldn't take it anymore and did call the doctor. They gave me an appointment to come in with Marie that afternoon. We continually watched Marie throw up and held her and did the best we could to comfort her. Marie did not have a fever so I didn't know what kind of illness she had. Usually, with a virus, you get fever but not always.

I took her to the doctor later that afternoon, and the doctor said it is still a virus and time will heal it and to just ride it out. The doctor explained again many children were coming down with this stomach virus and Marie has the same symptoms as the others. When I questioned the duration, the doctor again said this is normal. I took Marie home and fed her through the feeding tube. Thank God, we have it so we can keep her hydrated and nourished.

Day 6, Marie was still throwing up and getting so weak and tired. We had hooked her up to the feeding tube so she could get her formula gradually as we thought this may help. We usually just gave her feedings by putting eight ounces directly into her feeding tube, but nurse Jill said maybe if we feed her as an IV would, it wouldn't be delivered so fast in her stomach and upset her stomach as much. After trying to feed her the IV way, Marie tolerated her feeding for a few hours and then began throwing up again. I had been up all night with Marie due to her being so sick and weak; I held her most of the night. I went to take a nap to just get a couple of hours of rest before I had to get up and take care of Marie. I wasn't lying down for more than ten minutes when I heard the nurse Jill screaming. I ran into Marie's room and Jill was yelling, "Marie just threw up all over the bed and she is a mess." I was shocked at what I saw. Jill had grabbed Marie out of the bed, threw her in her arms, and brought her over to the rocking chair in her room. Jill then said to me, "This is crazy. She has to stop throwing up." I then realized how frustrated Jill had become with the whole situation. I started to clean Marie up while Jill was holding her. I was getting upset with Jill and yelled at her in my frustration. I yelled at her saying, "Jill, this isn't Marie's fault. You can't get this upset at her. Marie can't help getting sick!" I looked at Jill and she just looked so mad and sick of the whole thing. I told Jill to give Marie to me and go downstairs and take a break for a while. Steve had come in after hearing us and asked me what the matter was now. I told Steve that Jill is getting really frustrated and threw Marie, and I don't need this additional problem. Steve said we both needed to calm down and take a break. He then finished cleaning Marie's bed and I went downstairs with Marie in my arms to talk to nurse Jill. I explained to her I was upset about Marie too, but she didn't need to throw Marie like she did in the bed and get ticked off at her. Jill said, "She didn't mean to but was so frustrated and sick of Marie being like this and picking up the throw up all the time and it's ruining the carpet." I told her, "I don't care about the carpet or anything else Marie ruins, objects don't mean anything to me, Marie does." Jill did feel remorse about throwing Marie out of the bed. When I say throwing Marie, I don't mean literally but did toss her a little to the end of the bed to get her out of the throw up and then threw her in her arms to get her out of bed. I just never saw anyone get so upset with Marie, and it was really difficult for me to watch this behavior. Jill went home as I told her to go relax and we would see her tomorrow and that she needed a break from us.

I called Marie's neurologist and asked if the new medication could have anything to do with Marie getting so sick to her stomach if this was a side effect. The doctor had said no and that he had never heard of stomach upset to be a side effect of Baclofen. So I wasn't getting anywhere as to what was happening to Marie and what was the cause of the condition she was in.

Day 7 came and Marie continued to throw up again and we still were feeding her by IV instead of directly and giving her Pedialyte for extra fluids. I received a call from the neurologist who we saw out of state and she told us she wanted us to go and see a doctor who was a geneticist. I agreed to see the geneticist and she told us she didn't have any answers to Marie as far as the diagnosis for her condition. I then asked this neurologist if she knew about any side effects that may appear in patients taking Baclofen as Marie was now taking this drug. I told her how Marie was so sick—sick to her stomach all the time. The doctor informed me that she had heard or knew of Baclofen can make patients taking it sick to their stomach. After hanging up the phone and thanking the doctor for all her past help, I began to think about what she said about the side effects of the drug Marie was on. I told Steve that this was a side effect and we should pursue the doctor to doing something. Steve agreed. Marie was still getting really weaker and weaker by the day. We didn't know what to do.

The following morning, now day 8, I decided after Marie threw up a couple of times and been up all night to go to the emergency room. Nurse Jill arrived and I told her I was taking Marie to the hospital. Jill went with me and the doctor at the emergency asked what the matter was. I told him Marie had been throwing up for about a week now and we don't know why. Jill was as sweet to Marie as she lay in the hospital bed all snuggled her up so close to her. The nurse at the hospital said, "Marie looks so comfortable all snuggled up in your arms." Jill had wrapped and held Marie close to her in the bed. Marie was happiest when you held her or rocked her. She cried after each time she threw up and you just wanted to hold her and make it stop. The nurse had given Marie fluids and ran some blood work as the doctor instructed her to. The test had come back negative for any type of answers as to why she was so sick. I explained to the doctor how I called all Marie's doctors and what they had told me about her condition. After about three or four hours went by and no answers for Marie, the doctors decided to admit her for observation. Marie went to the seventh floor in the hospital where she usually went. Some of the nurses recognized her and told us how big she had become and how tall she was now. Marie was always that tall lanky child and still thin and even more so now. When Marie was in her hospital room, she began throwing up again after a feeding and the doctors were called. The doctors still did not know the cause. I was getting frantic by now, to say the least, and had to do something. Jill went home after staying with us all day. I told Jill I would call her and let her know how Marie was doing, and Jill was going to watch Marie in the morning so I could just go home to see Joe before he went to school. The night went on and the nurse kept giving Marie her fluids and did her medication as she normally gets them. Steve stayed at the hospital late in the night until he had to go home to take care of Joe and go to work in the morning. I stayed with Marie all night and Jill was trying to get into the hospital, but the visitor's desk wouldn't let her in until 9:00 a.m., saying that was visiting hours. I tried to explain to the visitor's desk that Jill was there as Marie's nurse and going to relieve me to take care of my daughter on the seventh floor. Well, they didn't care and wouldn't go against policy so we had to wait until visitors' hours. I had to then get Steve to stay and wait to go to his work and told him to put Joe on the school bus when it comes at 8:30 a.m. Everything worked out, problem solved on scheduling for the morning, a little inconvenient but problem solved.

Jill was then allowed to come up and she did stay with Marie. Jill also notified me that she was not going to be able to stay with Marie at the hospital to be her nurse as the agency she works for doesn't allow it. Which I could understand. Marie did have nursing care at the hospital, not every minute or hour but nursing care. Jill not being able to be there means I would have to be there all the time to watch Marie. I always stayed with Marie due to the fact I didn't trust the hospital in case of any slipups. We had seen them in the past. I, unconsciously, think I never trusted doctors or nurses. Not that I think they would intentionally harm my daughter but because they are so busy and so rushed things get forgotten. Many times, hours would go by and I would have to remind nurses of Marie's medication that it was due to be given and which ones, because they had forgotten her and they were extremely busy.

I went home after Jill said she would stay with Marie for a while and said she could only watch her today (due to the nursing agency's policy). I went home and the first thing I did was call Marie's pediatrician and asked him if there was something we were missing. I also asked him to call Marie's gastroenterologist (which was her feeding tube or stomach doctor as we called him); the doctor said he would but didn't think the gastroenterologist could help either. I told him I already tried calling that doctor, but the nurse said he was busy and would call me back. I also told the nurse in the gastroenterologist's office that Marie was in the children's hospital which the doctor worked from. I hung up from Marie's pediatrician and had still not accomplished anything to help Marie.

Neither doctor called me back so I took a shower, let the dogs out, called Steve, and then went back to the hospital to be with Marie. Jill was there and watched Marie just sleeping all the time I was gone. Jill left and I told her I would call her and let her know how things were going. Jill had told me that she was going to be working during the day at a nursing job she did on the weekends, so I could call her on her cell or at night at home. Jill left and Marie's grandparents came to see her. They were as worried about her as they always are. Marie's gastroenterologist came walking in the door of her hospital room. After greeting us, he asked me why he was not told of any of Marie's condition and why no one had bothered to call him. I told him I just did and I really didn't think of him until early this morning. His name is Dr. R., and he has a great sense of humor and said to me, "Well, thank you for finally thinking of me. Didn't anyone think I may know what is wrong with Marie? I am her gastroenterologist." I just laughed at him and said, "Sorry, it just didn't occur to me." He said, "Well, why didn't I get a call from any of the doctors?" I said I didn't know that one either. So he began to go over every detail with us and examined Marie. He then said he didn't know but was willing to do some tests. He ordered test and x-rays and nothing showed up there either.

Marie continued to throw up in the hospital and they were giving her something for the nausea to help her. The medication didn't stop the throwing up but seemed to help a little bit. It was day 8 in the hospital with Marie, and the doctors said she could go home and give the antinausea medication time to work and see if that helps.

Marie went home and continued to throw up. I called her neurologist and asked if he thought it might be the Baclofen, he said, "No, he didn't think so." I felt so frustrated and tired and not sure again what to do and with no ending insight to this nightmare, Marie was in again. Jill came the day after Marie came home from the hospital. I had decided that I was going to take Marie off the new medication Baclofen to see if Marie was feeling the side effects of the newest drug that we had given her, after which all this started. I began to think about other drugs which took sometimes a month or two to show side effects and I also thought about the other out of state doctor telling me she heard of Baclofen having side effects which made patients sick to their stomach. So after telling Steve, I didn't give Marie her morning dose and was going to see if she began to improve.

I told Jill what I was going to do in regard to the medication and told her I didn't give her the morning dose. I also told Jill to hold off on giving her the afternoon dose. I would give her the nightly dose since I knew I had to wean her off the drug and not take it off suddenly. Marie was doing pretty well. Her morning feeding stayed down and she was not throwing up for the first time in weeks. Jill had blown a fit when she, I guess, thought about what I was doing with the meds and said, "I couldn't just go off the medication and she would not stop the afternoon dose without orders from a doctor." I was so frustrated and told her, "Do what you have to do. I don't want Marie to have that medication. I wanted to see if she comes around." I went about the house and did some work and was busy doing whatever I had to since no house work had been done while Marie was in the hospital. Jill had told me her supervisor was coming to the house today to check on things with Marie. I didn't think anything of the visit from the nurse as they usually came once a month to check on the nurses and the patient in the care of the nurse.

The supervisor came in an hour after Jill had told me she was coming which I was surprised she came that quickly. Jill told me she was here and they would like to speak to me. The supervisor said as she was sitting at our table, "What is going on here?" I said to her, "What do you mean?" She then explained, she said, "Jill tells me that you are dropping Marie's, medication Baclofen." To which I said, "Yes, I am. I believe that this may be the cause of Marie's illness." Then things began to get really tense as I began to realize what this visit was all about. The supervisor began to tell me how I looked tired and am not thinking straight and not treating Marie with good judgment. Jill had told her that I was just not dealing with this correctly and I had no idea what I was doing. To which I replied, "No, I don't, but it is better than just letting her keep going as Marie was and I was told by a doctor this could be a side effect and I was going to see." Jill in the meantime, while Marie was in the hospital, had taken a position which she worked on the weekends and was offered more money as she told me that morning. I told the supervisor I was going to continue with my plan of decreasing Marie's Baclofen regardless of what she said. The supervisor then called Marie's neurologist and told them of my plan as I was standing there. I felt like I was a victim and being violated by my rights to take care of my daughter and as if I was a total incompetent mother. The supervisor then got off the phone and recited to Jill what medication was to be given to Marie and the Baclofen was to stay on. I became irate, to say the least, and said, "You are not giving my daughter that medication. I won't allow it!" She then said, "Oh yes, we are, and you will have to deal with it." She said, "You are not a doctor and cannot take medication off when you want to!" I responded to her by saying, "I will take her off the medication, and you can both get out if you don't like it!" I had told the supervisor how Jill had thrown Marie and she was becoming frustrated with Marie and I know she loved Marie, but I thought she had been getting tired of Marie being sick all the time. Well, they both left after I had thrown them out and I felt so helpless, humiliated and like a victim of their badgering.

Jill had left and I thought now what am I going to do? Steve came home from work and I explained what just transpired and he was shocked. His reaction was as he said, "The hell with them, you are going to do what is best for our daughter, no matter what they think." I said "Yeah, you're right. The hell with it. We will have to get another nurse now."

Marie began to feel better just that day. She had only thrown up once but was doing better. I decided I just couldn't give her the Baclofen anymore because she was doing so well. That night, she slept right through. She was so tired but didn't throw up. I got my first night of sleep after weeks of not sleeping well and even staying awake all night to hold Marie. The next morning, I woke up and it was like Marie was back to herself. She looked good when

I went to see her in her bed sleeping soundly with color back in her.

Marie woke up. I fed her in her tube and after a couple of hours. she didn't even throw up. I even took her off the nausea pills the hospital had given her to see if she could withstand not having those pills. Steve came home from work and I told him Marie didn't throw up at all today and was feeling better.

Steve looked at her and knew right off the bat she was back to herself. Steve then said, "What do you want to do about Jill, the nurse?" To which I said, "I didn't know. Why don't you call her and see how Jill feels?" Steve called Jill and she said I accused her of things like throwing Marie and she said she did throw Marie but was just so frustrated and she didn't think I was dealing with things in the right way. Steve said to me, "Why don't you call Jill since you're the one who threw her out and got rid of another nurse we had?" Ouch! That hurt, but he was right. I knew that the Jill thing would come back and bite me when things calmed down. He usually did bring things up after I made a rash decision. Not that I made rash decisions very often but I did know Marie, and I was going to do everything on this earth to save her at whatever the cost. My reputation as a mother was very good. The doctors never judged my competence as a mother, and they knew I was not going to quit on whatever the issue was that pertained to Marie's health. Although the doctor was not supportive in my decision to go off the medication, I did it anyway and Marie was better every day and did not throw up again. I informed the neurologist office that she was better after a few days went by and they admitted it must have been the Baclofen that caused all the problems she had been having in the past weeks. I had been holding my breath the whole time, practically, that Marie had not taken the Baclofen because I was not sure this was really the cause. It turned out that, thank you, God, again I had been right. The medication was out of her system and she was back to herself.

Marie went back to school the following week without a nurse. We called the agency asking for another nurse and told them we didn't think Jill would come back. The nursing agency had told me she had given her notice to quit and that she had already taken a job while Marie was in the hospital. The nursing agency said they would have the supervising nurse who came to my house a week ago call me. The supervisor nurse called me and we spoke and she told me again how Jill gave her notice to their agency. I told her I thought Jill was looking for another job because she had become frustrated with me and the way I was handling Marie's illness, and I also told them the other position Jill took offered her more money and she had wanted to go. The supervisor then told me she was sorry she had no idea that this was going on that Jill made her a victim to her scheme of looking for a way out of being Marie's nurse to work for more money. The supervisor said she worked for another agency also and would give them my name if I wanted them to find a nurse for Marie. I agreed to go with the other agency since she said they have more nurses and highly qualified.

Our search began for a new nurse and started with a new nursing agency. It was now the beginning of May and Marie was doing well and feeling well. May came and still no nurse for Marie, but we managed. I was back at work and things were back to normal or as normal as they could be without a nurse.

The New Nurse

It was the end of June and summer was approaching. The kids were out of school and I was home and just working part time at the summer camp. I received a call from the new agency and they found a new nurse for Marie. I did explain to the agency my situation with the old nurse and why we lost the last one to let them know just what kind of mother I was. I didn't want the same thing to happen again and wanted to let them know I was fully in charge. I know they have their rules but as I told the agency, "I will take care of my daughter's ups and downs as they may occur and do quite frequently and if it meant they didn't trust my decision, they would leave too." I explained Marie is not your ordinary handicapped child and has no diagnosis, and she will throw you for a loop every once in awhile and the new nurse must be able to handle it. I am learning, like I said to be very precise and aggressive, but in an educated way to deal with professionals or caretakers in regard to my precious daughter, for whom, I would give my life.

With all this said and done, the new nurse is coming out to our house today, June 30, 2007. Marie, since she had a birthday in May, is now seven years old and weighs about forty-five pounds. The new nurse comes in with the supervisor and she is a little older than I expected. Marie is sitting up in her chair with us as we go over all her routines and medications. The nurse turns and talks to Marie and tries to take her hand. I then explained, "Marie doesn't like it when people grab her left hand. You can touch her on her other hand. She won't pull away then." The nurse had told me she noticed Marie doesn't like it when she does that. I told her the doctors think she had a stroke on the left side and not sure when and that's why Marie doesn't use the left side especially her hands and arm. The nurse said she thought Marie was very pretty and is very cute. The supervisor then left and the new nurse stayed and I explained all about Marie's routines and told her schedule. The new nurse, whom I'll call her nurse "D", was very direct and completely competent. I could tell right away. I knew she would love Marie and take good care of her as she seems like a grandmother.

Nurse "D" began working the next day and fit in very well and was able to do the job of taking care of Marie. She went to summer school in the town we live in with Marie as scheduled the next day. She called the bus company and made sure they were picking up Marie and had everything ready to go for school the following day.

Things were going well. Marie was in summer school and the new nurse was adapting and learning all about Marie's likes and dislikes. They became like two buddies, Nurse "D" protected her like she was her own and never let anyone do anything at school that Marie didn't want them to do. Nurse "D" also had a way of pushing Marie to do more things she knew she could do but was kind of too lazy or didn't want to be bothered doing but made her do. We were relieved to know Marie was in good hands as long as nurse "D" had her in her care.

The summer flew by and Marie was finished with summer school by August 3. Joe was enjoying the summer too since he loved being out of school. Joe was due to go away with his grandparents for a week on vacation. We were a little apprehensive of letting him go away from us for a week because this was the first time he would be away so far and for so long from us. Marie had her nurse to keep her busy and loved her walks in the summer weather. We stayed at home this summer. We never went anywhere on vacation with Marie's condition except for when we went to my mother's old beach house. My brother owned the beach house now so we never went there anymore.

August went by and everything was good, the kids were good and life was good.

School started and Marie was going into second grade and Joe was going into first grade. Nurse "D" was going to school with Marie to protect her and care for her the way she did so fabulously.

The next six months went by and life was as normal as it could be for Marie. She had her occasional ear infections and colds, but things were uneventful.

Marie Needed Surgery Again

It was now February 2007. We were due to go to Marie's orthopedic appointment. This was the doctor who kept track of her bone ailments. Marie had seen this doctor since she was one year old. The orthopedic doctor was extremely kind and was great with Marie. She had been watching and taking x-rays of Marie's hips because they had been gradually coming out of her hip socket (this is in real layman's terms). The doctor said it was time to operate. Marie's hips were in immediate need of surgery and couldn't be delayed any longer as they were deteriorating drastically. The orthopedic doctor explained to me that in order to line the hips and correct the bones, Marie would have to be in a cast for four to six weeks. I was shocked but figured we have to do what we have to do. So we left with the intention of having the surgery and waited for the next available appointment for her operation.

It was a week later after the orthopedic doctor's appointment when we received a call from the doctor's office and they said the next appointment available was March 8, 2007. We made the appointment and waited for the day to come. The month went by fast and I tried to get some things done at our house to make it easier on Marie.

The day before Marie's surgery, we arranged for Joe to stay with his grandparents and packed him for a few days. We were not sure how long Marie would have to stay in the hospital. The doctor said four to six days. I packed Marie with all her favorite blankets and comfortable pajamas. I had to pack for me too since I was going to be staying with Marie during her hospital stay. It was late in the night when I finally finished and had everything packed. I went to bed and tried to sleep, but Steve and I could not sleep because we worried about Marie's surgery.

The morning came and we had to be at the hospital early at 8:00 a.m. for her hip surgery. We arrived and the nurses took Marie into the prep room and got her ready for her surgery. We had to fill out paperwork. The doctor performing the surgery—her orthopedic doctor—came in the room and explained everything. I was a little shocked when I asked her about the cast Marie would have and she told me then Marie would be in a full body cast to be sure she doesn't move the hip bones at all because the bones needed to set. The surgery would take four to six hours, the doctor told us. After the doctor was done explaining, she said she was ready to begin. The nurses told us one, Steve or I could go in the room where she would be and see her before she goes into surgery. I told Steve he could go. I just wanted it to be over with and didn't want to see her before she went in for fear I would break down and cry and not let her go. Steve went in the room before she was to go for her surgery. He kissed her and told her to be well. When Steve came out of the operating room, he looked relieved and scared at the same time. We walked over to the room where the nurses told us to wait in this family recovery waiting room. Each hour went by so slowly and it felt like days went by as we waited to hear from the doctor. I was too nervous to even read but tried to keep busy reading one of my college books. Steve just stayed quiet and tried reading a magazine to keep occupied too as we waited.

After about four hours sitting in the waiting room, the doctor finally came and told us everything went well. The doctor said they finished earlier than they thought because she had another doctor helping her do the surgery on Marie's hip. The doctor said she did one hip and another doctor did the other hip bone to put it back in place and put a new socket in. Marie also had to have metal plates put in each hip to keep the ball in her hip from pushing out the way her hip was pushing out. The doctor showed us to where Marie was recovering. I took one look at her and saw how pale she looked and drained from the surgery. Marie was sound asleep and didn't seem to be in pain. The doctor said she would probably not feel the pain until the anesthesia wore off. They would keep her on pain medication as long as she would need it. The doctor then showed us under the sheet what the cast looked like. All I could say was, "Oh my god, I had no Idea she was going to be like this!" Marie had a bright pink cast that went from five inches under her neck and went all the way to the top of her toes. She looked like a pink mummy. It was all I could think of. Steve was in shock too. I don't think he got a word out until he said, "Oh, well. We'll just have to deal with this." I felt so bad for Marie because I knew in the weeks ahead, she would not be able to move and could not roll over on her side to sleep as she always did. No matter what side you put her on at night to sleep, she woke up in the morning on the other. She also loved to have a big stretch in the morning when she woke and let you know she was ready to get up. Marie also liked to sit up in bed to let you know to come and see her and that she needed something. I knew she wasn't going to be able to sit up for four to six weeks or to do all the things she loved to do. Life was limited as it was for Marie, so it broke our hearts to take anything she had away from her. We knew we had to do this and get through it for Marie.

Marie was wheeled up to a room, of course, on the floor where she always went and again the nurses and aides remembered her. It was late in the afternoon by the time she was settled into her room. I told Steve to go home and see Joe and let him know his sister was okay. I think Joe was a little worried about his sister because he had asked Steve and me so many questions the night before at home. Marie slept and slept through the night; she let out whimpers as she was in pain. The nurses gave her pain medication which comforted her until the pain medication wore off again. Marie had to keep getting pain medication. She didn't really wake up until the third day and they got her up for a little while after surgery but she just slept. The nurses and I would move her onto this big long metal wheelchair it looked like a wheelchair of some type from the 1950s. The wheelchair was all she could go in and lay flat out, and we could prop her up to feed her with pillows behind her back and neck.

After about four days, it was Sunday, Marie was more alert but still sleepy and in pain. We were hoping we could take her home but a doctor covering orthopedics; actually it was the doctor who helped Marie's doctor do the surgery, came in to see her. He told us Marie could maybe go home tomorrow but definitely not today. Joe came to see Marie again and we showed Marie that Joe was there, but she was too tired to see him. Joe was anxious to see her so Steve's parents brought Joe in. Joe liked signing her cast and thought it was funny. Marie had this shocking bright pink cast from head to toe. Joe said, "Can I sign my name on her cast and put Sam, Mally, Periwinkle, Mocha and Percy's signature on, too?" Steve told Joe, "Sure! I think Marie would love to have all of them on her cast." Our dogs and cats were the names of the pets we had that Joe wanted to put on Marie's cast. Marie slept and ate a little bit. We took Joe to dinner across the street from the hospital, which was a great relief and nice to have Joe's company for a while. We came back to Marie's hospital room and Joe left with his grandparents. Steve's parents were always so thoughtful and helpful and they offered to stay with Marie so we could have the time with Joe and we could visit with him for a little while and have dinner with him. I stayed with Marie so I hardly ever got to see Joe.

Marie had to stay in the hospital for about six days, and we finally were allowed to take her home on March 13, 2007. Marie was still very weak and tired but gained in her strength as the days went on. We took her home and tried to maneuver her around the best we could. The hospital had given us this big huge metal wheelchair; it looked like a wheelchair from the 1950s.

We were due to leave the hospital and realized we couldn't fit Marie in my van because I had a smaller van. The nurse told us we could have an ambulance transport her home. We decided that was a great idea since we didn't have any other way. I had waited three hours when the ambulance had finally come to take Marie home. The EMTs who were there to take Marie were two young guys and were strong enough. They had such a difficult time getting Marie out of the bed and on to the stretcher; I thought they were going to break her bones more while trying to move poor Marie. I didn't want to be insulting but finally after multiple attempts by them, I told them to each grab a leg and I would take the front of her and we got her on the stretcher. Marie just looked around as she was wondering what the EMTs were doing. We were going down the hall to leave and saying good-bye to the nurses in the meantime. These two EMTs were banging Marie in to everything from wall to wall. I was a nervous wreck by the time we got to the elevators and getting into the elevator, Marie nearly flew off the stretcher. The EMTs kept apologizing and told me that one was new and was in training. I thought, *Really, I'm so surprised, you seem like you know completely what the hell your doing*! We got out of the elevator and to the ambulance, and Marie almost fell off the stretcher again. I thought this ride would never end and we would be home. We only lived about fifteen minutes away from the hospital. We did get home and Steve came out and asked me, "What the hell took you guys so long? You told me you were on the way forty-five minutes ago?" To which I told him, "We have EMTs in training and it's not going well. Just carry Marie in and let them get out of here!" Steve went and picked up Marie and carried her to her room so she could rest. The EMTs left and I thanked them for the pleasant ride. They had said they hoped they didn't scare me too much. I said, "Oh, no. Not at all, it was great, see ya."

Marie slept through the night and her nurse came in the morning and immediately began attending to Marie's needs. We decided we would move Marie out to our family room and put her in the wheelchair. We each grabbed one end of Marie to carry her out to the family room. She was so heavy with the cast and she was at an angle so awkward we had to be careful how we maneuvered her in the doors and watch out for the walls to not bang Marie. We had to move Marie every two to three hours so she wouldn't get stiff from sitting in one spot. So we did this routine of carrying her back and forth each day to let Marie watch TV and move to a different room. Marie looked like a mummy and you could see her watching us each time we carried her and wondering if we would drop her or bang her into something.

I went back to work and had to come home on my lunch hour because Marie needed to be moved and the nurse could not lift Marie because, of course, she was too heavy in the cast. So we had this routine down to a science by the first few days and continued until the cast was to come off.

Marie was tolerating the cast very well. I was getting a bit crabby by the third or fourth week of the cast. Trying to keep the cast clean was a mission in itself. Not to gross you out, but the "bathroom" of her cast was getting impossible to clean. We had used baking soda and tried everything to keep the cast clean. I knew I had to keep going at least another week so I could only wait and hope for the day the cast came off Marie.

The last week went by quickly and Marie was getting the cast off. It was April 13th. We went to the appointment and had to go take Marie to x-ray first. We did the x-rays and that was challenging as we had to move her in a small x-ray room. We got the x-rays done and got to see the doctor to have the cast removed. The doctor, I was told, was in surgery but the assistant would see us. We got in the room and the assistant told us he was not sure that the cast can come off today, due to the fact, the doctor wasn't there to approve the removal. I almost flipped out and said to the assistant, "This cast has to come off. The doctor said she would take it off this week. "I had called the doctor the previous week asking her to take it off then and she said she'll think about it and probably next week. So I sort of bent the truth when I told him the assistant that she would definitely take the cast off Marie today. I was so desperate and couldn't handle the cast on Marie anymore. Marie was doing fine but it was wearing on me and Steve, especially the nights when we had to switch her to her side and readjust all her pillows during the night as she would get cramped staying in one position for long periods of time.

The assistant doctor said he would call the doctor and send her the x-ray and see what she said. I told Steve that, "This cast better come off or you will have to drop me off at the nearest mental institution. I can't take another day of Marie in this cast." Steve said, "Just see what happens, maybe the doctor will tell him it can come off." I think Steve was thinking I hope they do take the cast off or Julie's going to go into one of her rampages and flip out again.

After a few minutes, the doctor's assistant said the doctor thought the x-rays looked good and Marie was healing fine and the cast could come off. The assistant removed the cast and Marie let out a scream and crying and shivering all at the same time like I never saw or heard her before. The doctor said she was crying because she was freezing and was having muscle spasms which were giving her severe pain.

We quickly grabbed all the blankets we could find and wrapped Marie in them. She was so cold because, as the doctor explained, she was use to being wrapped in the cast for the past four weeks and she was kept warm in the cast. She was like a baby coming out of a mother's womb. We had to dress Marie and it was so painful for her but we rushed and she was a little warmer but still having the muscle spasms and in a lot of pain. The assistant went to get Tylenol to give Marie and that seemed to help her a little. I felt terrible because I had pushed so hard to get the cast off. I had no idea she would be in so much discomfort. I certainly would not have made the doctor take the cast off and they wouldn't if she was not healed well or at all.

We took Marie home and bundled her up and gave her muscle-relaxing medicine the hospital gave us and it seemed to have helped. Marie slept after we gave her the medication and seemed much more comfortable. Marie's nurse went home. It was a long day for her, too. She was so worried about Marie when she came out of the cast. Marie's nurse had helped Marie every minute from the time she came out of the cast and wrapped her and asked for pain medication for Marie right away. So it was a tough and exhausting time for the nurse, too.

Marie woke up the next morning still having the muscle spasms and in pain. I gave her Motrin to see if that would help with her pain and within a half hour, she was back to sleep again. As the day went on, Marie seemed to get better and the pain was letting up. Moving was still tough on her as it evoked the muscle spasms.

Each day for the next week, the spasms seemed to dissipate until they no longer gave her pain when she moved. I was so relieved to see her finally get better and not crying every time we moved her. The following week, Marie went back to school and doing her usual routine.

Having a Difficult Time Feeding

The last six months were normal and nothing out of the ordinary had happened. We did see a geneticist who told us Marie may have a rare type of chromosome. The geneticist we saw—who told us about the chromosome may be rare—was from out of state. He said he needed to run more tests and we would have to come up to see him again.

We went to see the geneticist and after running the last test, he thought Marie had a syndrome called Rett syndrome, and she resembled the physical and mental characteristics of the syndrome. The doctor then told us that the test did not prove to be Rett syndrome as he thought. It was funny because I had researched it and asked Marie's neurologist if he thought Marie may have Rett syndrome and he said no. "She had already been tested and the test then had proved negative. The new geneticist redid the Rett syndrome test because he said they had new type of testing for Rett's.

The geneticists had a son who worked with him also and he called his son in to look at Marie and asked his son, "What would you think looking at this little girl? What do you think she has?" His son answered, "Rett syndrome. She resembles Rett's characteristics."

The father of this doctor said, "No, she doesn't. She tests negative for Rett syndrome." The doctor continues to check Marie and said he couldn't find anything that sticks out. The doctor, the geneticist, said he wanted to look into the chromosome test. The doctor explained that he needed my blood to be tested. He told us what he was looking for and he explained it to us; he believed Marie had an extra chromosome and that if I didn't match her, then Marie would be the first person he had ever seen in this world. No one had it and she would go down in history and put in the history books of medical journals. What he meant was that the extra chromosome that Marie carried, if I matched her, then it really meant nothing and she would not be the only one possessing this extra chromosome. We were shocked, to say the least, and thought about it all the way home for two hours. We were excited to finally, maybe have an answer to something to do with Marie's condition. The doctor had told us it would probably take six to eight weeks to get my blood test back as they would screen it more carefully.

We waited for a month to pass and were so anxious for the results. Time seemed to go by so slowly. It was now October of 2007. The geneticist's secretary finally called two days later than the four weeks. She told me to hold while the doctor comes to the phone. I held my breath and waited for him to come to the phone. When he did, he told me that the test proved I matched Marie's chromosome count and that meant there was nothing rare about her chromosomes, we both matched. I was so disappointed because we had thought this was our answer. The geneticist said he would look into her birth more and see if he could find anything there that showed him any abnormalities. He asked me to send her records and I did. He also told me that maybe someone was trying to hide or did not disclose her birth records as I had been trying to get them to him for a few weeks now but the hospital said they couldn't find them and that all the records from that long ago, 1999, had been sent to a warehouse.

I finally received Marie's birth records from the hospital and asked them to send them to the geneticist out of state. The geneticist said he received them about a week later and he would look through them to see if he could see any of her birth abnormalities

The doctor called back two weeks later and said he couldn't find anything but to call a lawyer. I asked why. He said that they have people who look into baby births to see if there was any foul play. I really didn't know what he meant and had called the lawyer that he had given me the name of. The lawyer was of no help either. He said we needed grounds, I believe was the reason, but he couldn't help us. So much for that I thought and we were done with chasing that avenue.

We saw one more geneticist here in our state and he went through everything and couldn't find anything to give a diagnosis for Marie. We finally gave up and said that is the end of searching for a diagnosis for Marie. We would just have to accept this fact that we will never know what happened to Marie to make her the way she is today and for the rest of her life. We will just have to take whatever happens to her as it comes. Most people have a diagnosis, although the doctors say there are children out there who are undiagnosed with their disability. I have yet to find one as I work with many special education children and know the kids in my town and don't know of one who is not diagnosed. I don't mean to be so sour grapes, but I do get discouraged when we have no direction to follow because we don't know what Marie's syndrome is or her diagnosis. We don't have any prognosis as most parents have with their handicapped child to know which way their child will go in life.

I remember joining a support group for parents of special needs children. The support group was in the next town over from where we live. I knew some of the parents before and met some new parents of handicapped or special needs children I should say, to be politically correct. Anyway, I went to and dragged Steve to the support group also. We just couldn't relate to any of the other parents because most of their children were walking and talking. No one, thank God, had a child like Marie, who couldn't walk or speak, so the more they talked about how their Johnny did this today and their Susie did that, I just couldn't relate to them. As they were discussing where to have the next meeting, one lady said, "Why don't we have it start at your house?" Meaning our house. I looked at the group and said, "I was sorry but this is the end of the road for me, girls. I really can't relate to this group since my daughter is far more severely handicapped, and I'm glad you don't have a child like mine. Even so, we love her, she is so special to us, but I'm quitting the group." With that note, I left the group at the end of the session.

It was now November and I had to take Marie to get a swallow study. I called the doctor because I had noticed she was choking on her food and her juice for some time now. I thought each time she was having a bad day or just tired those days from having seizures when she did. I had an appointment for the next week to do the study with Marie. The study was just basically watching her eat food as the technician fed or I fed Marie. I had done this test before with Marie and always *hated* them for fear she would flunk the test, and she wouldn't have the ability to eat anymore. Marie usually passed as I said she has had this problem before with choking on food but 9 out of 10 times she passed.

So I took Marie to the test and my mother-in-law Dee came with me for the test. I had to go over with the technician her food intake, and she asked to see the foods I brought to put dye in the food. The technician was practically telling me to shove the food down Marie's throat while running the swallow test. The doctor who was running the test kept telling the technician to slow down. Then the technician was saying Marie was not swallowing and the doctor would say, "Yes, she is. I see the food going up in her nasal cavity and oh it's coming back down." After watching Marie swallow a couple of times, they said let's see how she drinks. So I gave her the juice and she started to choke and couldn't get it all the way down. The technician said, "Okay, that's enough." Marie clearly can't drink from that thing or at all." She went on to tell me Marie should not be drinking from the trainer cup and needed to be on a sippy cup. I thought and told her, "Duh lady, do you think we haven't tried to get Marie on a sippy cup?" We have tried for years and she would only go from bottle at five years old to this toddler nipple cup. Well, the test was over and the technician said I couldn't let her drink anymore. She clearly has a choking problem. I was just disappointed that I knew what she was saying was right. I just didn't want to hear it.

We left the test and I realized I didn't have Marie's cup and it was the only cup that works for her, and if she could ever drink again, she would need it. My mother-in-law said she would go back and get it. When my mother-in-law Dee went to get it, the technician told her, "I threw that cup out. She really should not drink out of that cup." I was really ticked off and went back and told her off and told her she doesn't know what she was talking about. Well, I guess I told her, and now I had ticked off another of the hospital personnel. I went home and called Marie's gastroenterologist who I thought was great, and he would tell me what he thought of the test.

After I explained what had happened, the gastroenterologist said to me, "Julie, do you want to know now what really happened in the swallow test today?" I said, "Yes, okay." He then told me, "Marie flunked and aspirated the whole time during the test." I said, "Well, no one told me. I fed her today. They just said I couldn't give her anything to drink but that was all." He said, "Well, they should have told you she aspirated, and who was the doctor running the test?" I told him I didn't know. I said to Marie's doctor, "So I can't feed her at all?" He said, "No, Julie. Nothing. I'm sorry but she can't eat anymore." I said, "Well, do you think it will come back to her, the ability to eat?" He said, "No, this has been coming for some time and I think the ability is just gone." The doctor knew he delivered a big blow to me and said he was sorry and knew how much it meant to me to have Marie eat and I had to accept that fact.

I hung up with the doctor and when Steve got home I told him the great news of the swallow test. Steve was disappointed, but he said he knew that was going to happen. She just wasn't eating right. Marie's nurse had been out on vacation and she was surprised to say the least when I told her Marie can't eat anymore because she was aspirating. Marie's nurse didn't believe it but had to go by doctor's orders and wouldn't feed her anymore.

So life went on and one more ability of Marie's was gone now too. We had to face it and did, although I had hoped it would come back.

November came and Thanksgiving was coming and I dreaded it because I knew Marie couldn't eat her favorite things. I knew we would have to eat and have her sit there and smell the food and watch us eat knowing she couldn't have any food. It killed me to think of it. When Thanksgiving came, I whined to Steve and said, "I'll just give Marie a little food." Steve said, "You better be careful. Do you want her to choke to death or aspirate? How thick can you be? The doctor said no food. What part didn't you get?" I said, "I got it." We sat down to dinner and of course, I took a little spoonful of mashed potatoes off my plate and gave them to Marie. She did okay, but by the second bite she started to choke, so I stopped. Steve said, "I can't believe you. Will you stop feeding her? She can't do it." I did stop, thinking all right, Steve; I'll stop till next time. Seriously, she could handle a little bite sometimes and do fine but you really had to give her a drop of food only on a good day and know when those days were. It was really nothing to fool around with and by no means did I want to give her food just to prove to everyone she could eat once in a great while. I may have given her something like cake that she loved maybe once every month and it was a half of a teaspoon if that and if she swallowed right away I knew she was okay. Sometimes, Marie would hold the food in her mouth and then eventually spit it out and not swallow it. I'm really not trying to gross you out. But just making my point of how I know when Marie could eat a bite or not. I had to confess to Marie's gastroenterologist when we had Marie's biannual appointment that I fed her from time to time. His response to my confession was, "No! Really, I would have never have known or suspected that." We both laughed. He knew me to well.

He also told me at that appointment he was leaving the state and going into a new practice. I was so sad and happy for him, but he was just a great doctor and had Marie since she was a baby. I said to him, "Now! Who will I be able to abuse once you're gone?" He said, "I'm sure you will abuse the next doctor who is taking my place." He told me all about the new doctor and how great she would be. He said, "You better leave her home though the new doctor is not going to have the time to give what she needs!" He meant Marie's nurse because she grilled him more than I did most of the time. I couldn't get a word in as she was asking him a hundred questions. He told me then to give him a hug and I did and wished him well in his new endeavor and told him I was happy for him.

We left the doctor's office and I was so down about the doctor no longer going to care for Marie. Well, we keep plugging along and go back to our daily routine. Marie was now in school and Joe, too.

It was now December 2007 and we had another appointment with the orthopedic doctor to check on the plates in Marie's hips. I asked the doctor if she could take the plates out because I thought they had to come out anyway and they stuck out of her skin. I thought maybe they bothered her, she never complained but just to know they were sticking out that much must bother her. The doctor said everything seemed okay with Marie's hips, although it was a bit early, usually they took them out in six months to a year. It had only been eight months. The doctor said it would be all right and she will make the appointment to do the surgery to take the plates out and give us the date.

The secretary called us back when we went home that afternoon after seeing the orthopedic doctor; she gave us the appointment for the hip surgery for Marie on December 13, 2007, to remove the plates from Marie's hips.

We waited for the day of surgery to come and it finally did and on December 13, as I said, she went in to have the plates removed. It was just a day surgery and the doctor said it would probably just take one and half to two hours and could go home after the surgery.

Marie went through the surgery and everything was fine. Marie was tired but didn't seem to be in any pain. We went home and let Marie sleep as she was tired and needed to rest. It was nighttime now and Marie seemed uncomfortable and in pain. We were not sure what could be bothering her except the surgery and the doctor said she may have a little pain, not a lot though.

The next morning came and Marie seemed very agitated and in pain. Her nurse came in that morning and we gave her Motrin thinking that may help her. Marie went back to sleep and the Motrin quieted her down. The day pretty much went on the same; Marie slept and woke for Motrin which seemed to help temporarily.

The next day, Marie seemed to be in more pain and cried when you moved her. I had to go to work and Marie's nurse was taking care of her all day. When I called home to check on Marie, her nurse thought we should call the doctor, that Marie shouldn't be in this much pain. The nurse called the orthopedic doctor's office and the receptionist said the doctor will call back, she was busy. The day went on and Marie was still in pain; this had been three days now after the surgery. Marie's nurse waited all day for a phone call and no return call. I came home from work and relieved Marie's nurse of her duty for the day. It was 7:00 p.m. And still no phone call from the doctor. The night Marie's pain seemed to increase as time went on and if we move to change her, she would whimper to let us know she was in pain. The night went the same as during the day. I tried holding Marie but that didn't seem to comfort her, it was almost more painful for her.

The next morning came and I had to go to work again and Marie's nurse was calling the doctor and demanding a phone response. The receptionist said to give her the pain pills and put heat on her hips to see if that would help. This was the advice given to her by the doctor's nurse. So Marie's nurse tried that and that may have helped a bit but not for long; within a half hour, she was really whimpering in pain. When I called home, Marie's nurse said Marie was in a lot of pain and she wasn't getting any relief from the pain medication. Meanwhile, I placed a call to the doctor's office saying Marie's in a tremendous amount of pain and what can we do or where is it coming from? I got nowhere because the doctor didn't call me back either, which was not like her.

The weekend had come and we just did everything we could to help Marie day and night. She was our whole focus. We had to take care of her every minute to help her with the pain. It was now Monday morning and the weekend was exhausting for Marie and us. We tried to keep the pain medication going and the Tylenol or Motrin seemed to help just a small amount with her pain. Marie's nurse came in and I told her, "I am talking to the doctor this morning if it takes me all day." I proceeded to call and demanded I get the doctor on the phone now and that my daughter was in pain.

A doctor's assistant came on or she was a nurse who was paged and said to try the heating pads again and they didn't know where the pain was. I asked for the doctor but was told I couldn't talk to her she was busy. The assistant told me if Marie was that bad then maybe I should bring her to the emergency room if the pain doesn't get better and told me to increase the dose of pain meds.

We did increase the pain medication, and that didn't seem to help but as long as we didn't touch Marie, she was okay lying in her bed. I had to go to work and went as I was late already. I called later in the day to check on Marie and the nurse said she was no better.

I went home from work at the end of the day and tried to console Marie by carrying her to the porch and rocking her. Marie seemed like she was trying to talk—almost trying to tell me to do something. I was rocking her and she was looking pale, and her breathing was labored as if she was having a difficult time trying to breathe. Steve had just come home from work and I told him what had happened and what the doctor's assistant had said earlier.

As I'm holding her, I called the pediatrician, not sure what to do. I had told the pediatrician's office that Marie seems to be having a difficult time breathing and I didn't know what else to do. I don't want to be one of these people who has a handicapped kid and brings her to the hospital every time I have a problem. I always keep this thought in mind. I hung up the phone with the doctor, and the doctor saying they didn't know what the matter was and call back if she gets worse. Like I said, I hung up the phone; I was holding Marie in my arms and she looked as if she was just going to pass out and then I said to Steve, "That's it. I'm calling an ambulance. I don't know what she is doing and I'm not risking her life anymore!" Steve called 911 and they were there instantly. The EMTs did notice Marie having a difficult time breathing and gave her oxygen right away; they also said she looked very pale. I explained what was going on and the surgery she had had a week ago. We quickly went off to the hospital to have Marie looked at. The emergency room was busy but they took Marie right away and an intern checked Marie out and noticed the pain and how her breathing was labored. The intern said we needed to have an x-ray done and so we did. When they moved Marie, I told the technicians, "Be careful, she's in a lot of pain, especially when you move her." The x-ray was over and we went back to the room they had Marie in. One of Marie's pediatricians had come in and I was crying when I told her what had happened in the last week. The doctor just hugged me and told her she is just having hard time breathing and she is better now with the oxygen on and her oxygen numbers were stabilizing. I told the doctor, "I feel so guilty, I should have never let things get this bad for Marie; she is in a lot of pain, and I don't know where it is bothering her!" The doctor said, "Oh, Mrs. Fargo, it's not your fault. Marie will be fine and get the care she needs here and be okay." She missed my point altogether, I wasn't worried about me to heal with my guilt. *Can you find the source of her pain, you idiot*, I thought. The intern at the emergency room told us they were going to put Marie in a room upstairs at the hospital and keep her in for observation. The doctor said her tests were okay—the blood test they had done—and so that was their plan.

We went up to a room on the seventh floor of the hospital and got Marie into another bed and it was killing

Marie to move her. The intern from the emergency room came in and I was so sick and tired.

I really didn't want to deal with anyone. Steve was there also and he was just as disgusted and frustrated as I was. The intern said, "We found the problem in the x-ray, Marie broke both her hip bones." We were shocked and said, "How did she do that?" The intern said, "Who knows. We don't know when or how but somewhere along after the surgery, she rebroke both hips." She looked at us like you didn't know this kid was in this much pain. "Hello." We told her we kept calling the doctor, but no one would put us through at the office and the nurses acting like Marie was nothing of importance. The intern said she had a call into Marie's orthopedic doctor and she would let us know when she heard from her. We were relieved that we now knew but really angry that Marie had to endure all that pain when someone could have helped her. Marie's orthopedic doctor's colleague had walked into Marie's room and explained who she was. The colleague said the doctor was going to be calling me any minute. I asked this doctor what we are going to do now. The doctor said, "I'm sorry all this happened, but we can't do anything for a while, a day or two." I was not taking that too lightly and said to the doctor, "You guys screwed this up and you need to fix it. It is inhumane to leave Marie in this much pain for another minute." I also said, "I will take Marie to another hospital if we have to tonight rather than leave her in this much pain." I was crying by now and felt so bad for poor Marie. The doctor looked at me and said, "We can't get her into surgery tonight. We couldn't even find an anesthesiologist or get an operating room and staff." I told her, "I don't give a damn what you have to do to get her some relief from her pain!" In the meantime, the phone was ringing and the nurse came in and asked me to pick it up; Marie's orthopedic doctor was on the phone. I picked it up and told her that Marie was in a lot of pain and her staff didn't help us at all. The doctor stated that she wasn't aware of Marie's condition at all and that no one informed her last week of Marie's condition. I said, "That was all well and good, but what can we do now for her tonight." The doctor told me we couldn't do anything until the morning and that they could give Marie heavy narcotics to sedate her and alleviate her pain through the morning. She said they would do the surgery in the morning and that she would grab every surgeon she could to get Marie's hips back in place. I had calmed down and the doctor's colleague was still in the room listening to my conversation with the doctor. I think she already knew or consulted with Marie's doctor already. She asked me if the plan was okay. We had no choice, we had to agree. Both doctors were very concerned and I knew they were deeply sympathetic to Marie's pain. I asked my husband if we were doing the right thing and he agreed. What choice do we have? The doctor gave the nurse the orders to keep the heavy medication to stop the pain and make Marie in an almost comatose state to help her through the night. They gave her the medication right away and Marie was fast asleep. I stood over Marie's bed and cried for her and said to her, "Marie, I'm so sorry, I didn't know how much pain you are in. You are such a tough little girl and you shouldn't have to bear this much pain." I felt awful and so did Steve. We had no idea that the hip surgery could be the cause. The doctor said she never heard of a child breaking both hips; one maybe but not two at the same time.

The next morning came, it was now December 20, 2008. Marie was due to go back into surgery to repair her hips. I was told she would need to have the full body cast put back on to keep the hips in place after the surgery. We didn't even care about the cast just as long as Marie was out of pain no matter what it took. Although in the back of my mind, I was dreading the cast again but I was willing to do anything at this point for Marie. We waited all day and finally about 8:00 p.m., they took her to surgery. We walked down to the operating room alongside Marie's bed. It looked like we were in a basement because we were and the preop room was so quiet and no one was around. The nurses kept calling out, "Hello, is anyone here?" Finally, a doctor came out and told us to go into this room. It looked like there had just been a party with desserts and food all on a table. I thought, *Oh this should be good. Where the hell are we? This is something out of the twilight zone.* The doctor was the anesthesiologist and asked us to fill out forms, really, just releasing the hospital if anything goes wrong in her surgery. Then Marie's doctor appeared and she explained everything as far as how the surgery was going to go and how long it would take. We knew it would be hours and the anesthesiologist told us to go home and not wait; the surgery would last well into the early morning by the time they finished. To which I thought, *Yeah, sure let me go out to have a fine dinner and I'll call you in the morning.* I wasn't going too far and told him so. I had to wait and would stay in her hospital room nearby and told them that's where I'll be. Steve and I thought we would quickly go across the street and grab something quick to eat as neither of us ate all day. We were too upset to eat for obvious reasons.

We were sitting there, both of us really not hungry, trying to force food down and trying to pass the time at a fast-food restaurant. We both said we needed a miracle but know those things don't happen too often with Marie. We finished eating. Steve went home and I went upstairs to Marie's hospital room to wait to hear anything about Marie's surgery. I was just reading and watching TV as time seemed to go so slow again.

It was around 11:00 p.m. when Marie's orthopedic doctor came in to Marie's hospital room where I was waiting. What she had told me next was incredible, she said, "I have good news and I have bad news, which do you want first?" I replied, "I'll take the good news. I don't think I could stand the bad right now." The doctors said, "The good news is she only broke one hip. The other hip that the plate was out previously was intact and her bone was fine. The x-rays showed her hip at an angle we couldn't see." I replied, "Oh my god, thank God it's only one hip that broke." That is the miracle we had been waiting for or said we might get. She then said the bad news is, "I couldn't make her cast any less than I did before; I had to do the full body cast to make sure she doesn't pull this hip out." I said, "Oh, that's okay. We'll deal with it. She does so great." After all I thought, "It's not about us or me it's about Marie." The doctor looked tired; she said earlier that she had been in surgery all day and looked tired. The doctor said she had to get back to help the other doctors to help finish with Marie's cast and she left. I thanked her and told her to go home and get some rest as soon as she could before she left the room. I knew the doctor had small children at home, and I felt guilty for making her stay as long as she already had for Marie's surgery. Both doctors had to get up early, the doctor's colleague also came in had told me earlier she had to go out of state in the morning and would see Marie later the next day.

Marie was wheeled in to her hospital room where I was waiting for her to come back from her surgery. It was about 1:00 a.m. when she finally came back to her room. The surgery was over. I thought, *What a relief.* Marie, when I looked at her, she looked pale but did not whimper from pain anymore. Marie had her bright neon pink cast on, the same color, same length as before from neck to toe in cast.

It was now December 23 and Marie was still so sleepy but managed to sit in a chair for a while; she was still in the hospital. We were hoping she would get out of the hospital today. The doctor had said maybe today. My mother-in-law, Dee, came in to stay with Marie so I could leave for awhile to go home and take a shower and go Christmas shopping.

I left the hospital and I needed to go to the mall quickly to grab a couple of gifts because I had no chance to shop for Christmas because of Marie being so ill weeks prior and her surgeries. I knew Marie was all right now and I could leave her with Dee. Marie just slept most of the time and we didn't have to get her up to feed her because she was being fed by feeding tube now.

I got home took a shower and ran to the mall and grabbed a few gifts and headed back to the hospital. Marie was still sleeping when I returned and Dee said she slept most of the time. I was gone maybe three hours at the most. Steve was now home from work and then would come to the hospital to get us whenever Marie was going to get discharged. It wasn't until about 5:00 p.m. when the doctor finally came in and said we could take her home.

Steve put Marie in my van and this time we were experts and knew how to lay her down on my bench seat of the van to get her home. We arrived home and Joe was happy to see Marie and the dogs were too as they jumped all over Marie to see her. Joe wanted to sign Marie's cast again so we let him design her new cast. We then settled Marie down on the special wheelchair that stretched out so she could layout in it and still prop her up a little. She enjoyed sitting up; it seemed and to be back home in her familiar surroundings.

I ran around the house trying to get Marie's hospital bed and room finished. Marie had to have the hospital bed put in because her bed couldn't position her up and down when she needed to. Her room was finally ready for her to go to sleep, so Steve moved her in and she did go right to sleep after her long day. It was tough for her just being moved to the car and in and out of places. I was still very nervous and when Steve would move her, I was constantly telling him, "Watch out the walls and watch out for the doors, you're going to bang her foot!" Steve was constantly saying, "I know, Julie. I am trying to be careful but you don't help by screaming at me each time to watch out for this and watch out for that!" We went through this dialogue the whole time Marie had each cast on.

Marie was sleeping and I had to make cookies and wrap two gifts for the morning. I like to go see two little handicapped girls I knew and tomorrow was my only chance and also it was Christmas Eve. I finished around one in the morning and had to go to bed. I was just beat and couldn't do anymore. So I went to bed but knew I or Steve would have to get up in two or three hours for Marie because we would have to flip her on the other side. Sometimes during the day or night, she may let you know she was uncomfortable and you would have to flip her over on her side.

We had to rotate her anyway so she wouldn't get bedsores. Changing her diaper as you may wonder was a challenge in itself. The doctor had to cut a hole in Marie's front and back to relieve herself and the doctor said, "Oh, and please try not to get the cast wet with pee or anything else from a bowel movement. I know this is a tall order, but it could make a mess of the cast and the cast will get pretty stinky." To which I said to her, "You have got to be kidding. How the hell are we supposed to keep the cast clean or clear of pee or poop for that matter when the kid can't even aim it?" This order was going to give me the most stress and it did.

It was Christmas Eve and Marie's nurse arrived and was shocked when she went in to see Marie in her full body cast. Nurse "D" right away began running around getting Marie up and I helped her move Marie onto the big long stretch wheelchair we had to use to lay her in. Marie was heavy and it took two people to move her except for her dad. He could move her now like a pro and did when I asked him to move her. We could prop her up to feed her and put her in front of the TV so she wouldn't get too bored. We had to move her back and forth every few hours so she wouldn't get cramped or have bedsores under the cast. At around 10:00 a.m., I left and ran around most of the day, going to see the two little girls who were handicapped to give them their gifts and see them. I dropped one gift off to one of the girls and then ran to the next little girl's house and was glad to see them. I had to rush out and run around to do more shopping. It was around 3:00 p.m. and I was trying to get to church for the 5:00 p.m. mass with Joe. I did everything I really needed to do and went to mass at 5:00 p.m. The church was packed and we barely fit in the church and stood in the back through the whole mass, if I had the time to get there a little earlier, as my husband so kindly

191

reminded me, I would have been able to sit and have a seat with Joe. It was still nice to go to Christmas mass with Joe as it will be a memory we will both have. I am so about memories. Steve tells me I'm crazy most of the time with my making memories ideas. Anyway, so we come home from mass and are supposed to be at Steve's moms and dad's house for Christmas Eve dinner. Joe is so excited and just loves going to Christmas at grandmas and grandpas and knows he will get spoiled ridiculously with toys. We had to get Marie to the in-laws, which was something out of a comedy show. My father-in-law was going to come over and we were going to transport Marie in his van to get Marie to the grandparents for Christmas Eve.

Well, it was six and I told Steve I'm still dressing Marie and trying to slip her Christmas dress over the top part of her cast which was not working too well. I finally got this damn dress over Marie and by this time freaking out because we're late and I can't get Marie dressed laying out in this cast and she had nothing to cover her feet and Joe was now running all over the house and getting the dogs all riled up. Joe decided he wanted to get something to drink and spilled the juice all over himself and was now all wet with juice and in his nice Christmas sweater and nice new pants. I told him to go change and dry the sweater and put it back on him and told him he can't eat or drink anything until we get to his grandmother's house. Joe's response was, "I didn't do it on purpose, the dog made me spill." It was always the dogs fault with Joe, never him. George, my father-in-law, showed up to take Marie to his house and Steve began emptying his van so the seats could be moved up and down to lay Marie down. Well, they figured out the seats, it didn't go down or up enough. I'm not sure but after emptying his van, we couldn't get Marie in. Poor Marie, Steve had carried her and put her in and moved her in every way trying to carefully stuff her into a spot in the van. Finally, he laid her out on the bench seat in the back of the van and we propped her up and stuffed pillows in front of her and in her back. It was like not to be insensitive but like trying to get a mannequin in a car that just wasn't going to go in easily if at all. I then got Joe to sit in the seat up ahead of me and I was getting in the seat just barely with Marie laid out behind me on the bench seat. Steve was following behind us in our van because he had to take the wheelchair and Christmas gifts because there was no room in my father-in-law's van. The grandparents lived about fifteen blocks away from our house. We probably could have taken the wheelchair down to their house and made better time. My father-in-law says as we are getting ready to leave, "This is stupid, I don't know why we have to go through all this. We should have not put Marie through all this hassle. This is ridiculous." When we started driving, I could not stay on the seat and just held Marie in the seat while I'm on the floor in the car and my arms holding Marie to keep her from not rolling forward. The hospital gave us this strap that we were supposed to use in the car bench seat to hold her in, but we couldn't get it to work. We got to my in-law's house and Steve said, as we are about to get out, he says, "I have to go back home. I forgot the pillows for Marie. We had certain pillows that fit her perfect in her wheelchair. Steve went back to our house and we had to wait in the freezing cold for Steve to come back to lift Marie in the grandparent's house. Steve was back quickly and brought Marie in the house and it was tough carrying her although her uncle helped but they had to go by eight or ten steps on the deck to get into the house. We put Marie in the wheelchair and she was okay and doing all right through it all. Everyone was happy to see her in the family and we were going to eat and Steve's mother after carrying on over Marie, with everyone sitting down for dinner, his mother said, "We could just wheel Marie in the living room in the next room right over here." Steve sees where she is telling him to go which is well in our view of her but didn't like her suggestion and says to his mother, "Mom, you want us to just wheel her in there and leave her there? What? Like she's some kind of object just put it there." She said, "No, I just meant there where you could see her." She just wasn't thinking about how she said just put her over there. Christmas Eve went great and Marie was tired. It was late and we needed to put her down to bed. We loaded both cars and went home the same ridiculous way we got there. We were all tired and the kids went to bed and Joe was excited for Santa to come the next morning. Steve and I had a lot to do for Christmas day to get ready for family to come and Santa. We went to bed around 2:00 a.m. and Joe was in our bed at 5:00 a.m., telling us to wake up to see what Santa left him. Joe was only six years old and I had to remember how important Christmas was for him. I asked him to give us a couple of more hours that Santa didn't come yet go back to sleep he'll be here in a couple of hours. Joe said, "No, I already looked and he left me toys. I saw all of them." I told him it was too early and go back to sleep when he jumped in our bed and rolled and tossed around till finally he got us up at 7:00 a.m. He was happy to then go downstairs and see what presents were left for him. I then got Marie up and Steve carried her into the room we call the porch which is now converted to a family room. Joe helped Marie see all her gifts Santa left her. We quickly got ready for my family to come and some friends for Christmas dinner at our house. At 3:00 p.m., every one began arriving and dinner went well. We managed to take care of Marie and take care of our guests, too. It was a great Christmas and we were happy to all be together.

The next few weeks went by and Marie's nurse continued to take care of Marie's every need. Nurse "D" was so kind and helped Marie get through this tough ordeal of this cast she had to put up with, and her nurse did everything possible to make Marie comfortable. I had to come home on my lunch hour to move Marie into her bed because I put her in the wheelchair in the morning with the nurse's help before I left to go to work. We had made the schedule that I would help her move Marie every day on my lunchtime and move her back at 3:00 p.m. when I came home. The schedule worked and the weeks were going by fairly quickly. Things were going well. I even could lift Marie myself when Steve wasn't around and was carrying her myself to her wheelchair. We had a friend and she was also a nurse's aide who came on Friday mornings to care for Marie; her name was Kathy. Kathy adores Marie and she takes great care of Marie. She also had to help lift Marie when she came in on Fridays and was a bit of a task for her to maneuver Marie and position her but she always managed to do it. The nurses both washed her and we had to find no rinse shampoo to have Marie's hair clean which was a challenge to wash her hair too, but the two nurses did it.

By the last two weeks, I was getting tired of this cast as Marie was too. I hated changing her diapers because it was always a mess that you were trying to not get the cast dirty which was impossible. It was getting hard for Marie to sleep and she had to be moved during the night. We never could get a good night's rest. It seemed like she wasn't comfortable no matter which way you put her on the left or right side. The poor girl couldn't even move to get in a good position during the night. I think she just wore herself out trying half the nights to get to sleep. In the last two weeks, I said to her, "I can't do this anymore. I am so tired of this cast and Marie is having a difficult time, too. I want it off!" Nurse "D" said to me, "Marie is doing so well. I don't think she minds half as much as you do." In other words and she looked at me as if she was saying get a grip, if she can deal with it, you certainly can, it's not about you, it's about Marie in the cast. So I shut up for the time being and continued to do what I needed to do and that was take care of Marie and Joe.

Marie got her cast removed on January 30, 2008, and we had to be very careful with her. She screamed with the cast coming off and was in pain again as the muscle spasms came. Marie was freezing too and we had to wrap her up quickly again and not move her so the spasms wouldn't come when she moved.

The doctor wanted to fit Marie for a hip brace because she didn't want Marie breaking her hip or doing any sudden moves right away. She would have to wear this brace two to three hours each day. We were due to go to Florida with Marie in a month, so we were nervous that she wouldn't make it for the trip. That is the next story.

Marie went back to school a week after her cast came off. I think the school was happy to have her back because they enjoyed having her there but also it made it easier for them. Marie had her tutor come to the house when she was out with her cast. Marie's occupational therapist and speech therapist also had come to the house to work with Marie while she was home in her cast. Everyone at her school was always so kind and generous to us and Marie when she was going through a difficult period in her life. When she was out with her surgery, her school teachers and the staff at the school sent meals and gifts home for Marie and us. The school called to check on Marie while she was out. Her friends in her class made cute get-well cards for Marie, and I read each one of them to her and still have them. They were so precious. The words the children wrote to express their thoughts to Marie showed how much they missed and cared for her. The school where I worked had also sent home meals for us and gift cards for restaurants to help us. My friends at the school I worked at were always there for me and my family. They never missed a time to help when I was in trouble with Marie; they always found some way to help us.

Life went on and everyone was back in their daily routine as we tried to get ready for some fun. Marie was not able to have physical therapy as she did at school and home for about three or four weeks for fear of pulling anything out or breaking any of the hip bones that were just repaired. We had to be careful how to pick her up and move her due to the plates in her hips were still setting. You could see the two metal plates bulging out from under Marie's skin because she was so thin and not much fat on her to protect her. We managed to be very careful and Marie's hip was mending each day.

Marie Is Going to Disney World

I had asked for Marie to have her wish granted. During the past summer, I had thought of asking Make-A-Wish Foundation to send Marie to Disney World. I had heard about Make-A-Wish Organization from other parents of handicapped kids who had gone with their children and thought after years I would see if Marie would get to go. In all honesty, I thought it was great for our family to go. I knew though we would need the help of an organization to get Marie to Disney as we couldn't get all her needs met in a hotel on our own. Make-A-Wish Foundation supplies everything you need and the place where you would stay is all geared for kids with special needs. So I applied. Marie's wish was to go to Disney. I picked this wish because Marie wouldn't enjoy anything else like they had children who meet their favorite singer or actor or actress. The children's wishes were to go to a special event but most wishes were to go to Disney, and I knew Marie would enjoy seeing all the Disney characters and out somewhere where the weather is warm for her and not too hot for her in February. I would love to go where it is real hot. The heat doesn't bother me, but it wasn't about me as I had to remember. (Really, I'm not that self-centered).

We received a call that Marie's wish had been granted. I knew the organization helped you get the child to their wish destiny but had no idea how wonderful and accommodating they would be to Marie's needs. The Make-A-Wish employee who called to tell me about granting Marie's wish said they would take care of everything. The girl I believe was named Karen and she said we could put Marie's wheelchair right on the plane. They would give us a handicapped van when we arrived in Florida. We would have a custom-built efficiency with special bathtub and many other amenities we would need. The place we would stay was called "Give Kids the World Village." A man who began this Give Kids the World started it from one-efficiency apartment for children who were very ill and didn't have the opportunity to go to places of pleasure. Karen told me the airlines would be informed of Marie's condition and that they would accommodate her on the plane. We also needed to bring her car seat so she could go in the van and we were told to just bring it and the airline would put it with luggage on the plane. Karen had told me two representatives would come to my house and give us the details and all our information when it got closer to the day of the trip. We had met the two representatives in the fall but we were so busy I couldn't really think of the trip to mention it and Marie was in such pain. I thought of getting the plates in her hip out in the fall, so going to Florida, the plates wouldn't bother her. I wanted her to have the best time with nothing to bother her.

So a couple of weeks went by and we were getting ready for the trip to Florida. The two reps from Make-A-Wish showed up. They had called earlier in the week and said they wanted to give us a party. The one representative worked as a teacher and her kids were having Marie's wish as their fundraiser for eighth graders. The teacher had asked me if she could come over and have a party with our family and the kids in her class wanted to send over gifts for Marie and Joe. The teacher had told me all the work the kids did, and I was amazed how they went from store to store and got donations and then went and bought gifts with the money for Marie's trip. The teacher had said the kids worked so hard and really she was proud of them. I said to the teacher, "Well, aren't the kids coming to our house also to the party?" She called this a bon voyage party that they always did at Make-A-Wish for kids before they went on their trip or wish as she explained to me. The teacher said to me in response to my question about the kids coming, she said, "Honest, the kids aren't coming. I wouldn't do that to you with that many kids to bring to your home." I said, "Well, why not? We would love to have them and meet them. They did all the work why shouldn't they be in on the party?" The teacher laughed and said, "No one has ever asked them to come to the party. I don't know. I guess if it is okay with you, they would love to come to your house." We arranged the time and hung up the phone and she said she would be out that Thursday. I thought, *Oh hell! My house is a mess*. It always was and we only cleaned when someone was coming. Joe always says, "Who's coming over?" when he sees me running around with the vacuum and dusting and throwing everything in closets that was not nailed to the floor. When Steve saw me running around like a nut, he asked, "What are you doing cleaning like a mad woman?" I told him we have about twenty to thirty kids coming over on Thursday. He said, "For what?" I then told him the great news he would love (haha). "The kids from the teacher's class who worked on Marie's trip were coming over for a bon voyage party and I invited them. He said, "You did what? Are you kidding me. What the hell did you do that for?" I said, "Steve, they did all the work and it would be nice to meet them and thank them. Why shouldn't they come and have pizza and cake and meet Marie?" Steve then calmed down. He also knew I would be going crazy for the next three days cleaning for them to come to our spotless house, yeah right!

The next three days flew by and it was now Thursday, 5:00 p.m., when we were scheduled to have our Make-A-Wish party. The door bell rang and it was the teacher who was running the Make-A-Wish party and the other representative. They had so many bags and pizzas and bags of gifts for Marie and Joe. I thought they would never stop unloading their cars. Then I looked out the door, there were cars lined up dropping off kids and the kids kept coming and coming. I thought to myself, *Oh my god! If these kids don't stop coming, Steve is going to kill me*. Marie's nurse was there also because she was coming to Disney World with us to take care of Marie in case anything serious happened to Marie. The nurse was letting the kids in and she was surprised at the number of kids that kept coming. I said to the nurse, "Are the kids still coming?" To which she said, "Yep! You asked for them so, here they are." I told her, "Steve is going to kill me. I told him just a couple of kids, not many." Steve's parents were also there because they were coming on the trip. They had to pay their own flight and didn't get all the tickets to the Disney events. We certainly understood why Make-A-Wish couldn't pay for everyone. It was nice that they were allowed to stay with us at the "Give Kids the World Village" where we would be staying.

So everyone was in and the kids all met Marie and gave Joe and Marie so many fabulous gifts for them to take to Florida. Joe was so excited; he was jumping around and just amazed. He said, "Mom, this is like having Christmas again." I said, "Yes, Joe. You are very lucky to have been given so many gifts." We had the pizza and they had a beautiful sheet cake made from a local bakery which was donated. The kids did so much work and we thanked them and told them how much we appreciated their great acts of kindness. The party ended and everyone left. Marie was exhausted from all the activities and everyone showing her all the wonderful gifts she had just received. We cleaned up every last bit of the party and went to bed. Joe was too excited to sleep as he had counted down on his calendar till we leave for Florida. It didn't seem real that he was actually going to Disney World until the party came and then he knew the trip was real. The week flew by and we were going to Florida the following Thursday which was February 28, 2008. We woke up that morning and everyone was running around. I had packed everyone the night before so I just had odds and ends to do. My odds and ends were usually major projects, so I ran around like a nut trying to get everything on the dining room table into luggage and still calling my in-laws asking them to give me more empty luggage bags because I couldn't fit everything for Marie in the fifteen other bags. We were going to be taken to the airport by limousines we were given two because we had seven people and Marie's wheelchair, car seat, and about twenty bags between us. The limousines showed up and I'm still packing and throw everything left on the table in one sweep of my hand into bags. The limo drivers were, I think, in shock to see all the stuff we had. This is why I would never attempt to take Marie ourselves since it would be impossible to have all the luxuries that were provided for us to go.

We left and got to the airport and went through baggage and through security. As we're going through security, the security officer told me I will have to wait with Marie and stay behind until another security guard comes. I had no idea that security had been so strict since 911 and I had not flown on a plane in years. I knew some of the rules, but I was ready to forget the whole trip when we tried to get Marie through security with her in her wheelchair. A female security guard came and checked Marie's wheelchair with Marie sitting in it. The female security guard said to me, "She doesn't have anything of danger on her does she? I wanted to say, "Yeah, sure. She has three machines guns, five pistols, and fifteen switchblades in the bottom of her wheelchair, you idiot!" Then I said, "No, she doesn't have anything on her that's dangerous." The female officer said, "Well, normally, I would have to do a strip search on her, but I'm pregnant and can't lift her much." I thought to myself well, thank God, but you are not strip-searching my daughter if I have to turn around and go home, I will, because you're not strip-searching her. Just because Marie was handicapped they were going to strip-search her, I thought this is a little extreme, 911 or not. I was in no way going to allow the security guards to do this strip search. I really was getting ticked off and everyone was waiting for us and could see I was really ticked off. I think I yelled over to Steve, "Sorry but I'm not doing this." He looked at me like, "What are you doing"? I was waiting for security to let us go or not but was not going to let them strip-search Marie. Finally, they let us go and security said she was fine; we didn't need to do the whole strip-search routine. We then joined the rest of the family and I told them what was going on and that we almost didn't come.

We boarded the plane. The airline steward and stewardess were so kind to Marie and let the people in wheelchairs go first onto the plane. I took Marie out of her wheelchair and the Stewart took her chair for me and put it in the plane. Everyone else boarded the plane and we all sat together. We were up in the plane and almost to Florida and Joe was so excited because this was also his first plane ride at six years old and of course Marie was eight years old. I was holding Marie in my lap or I should say Marie was sleeping in my lap. She had to get up a little earlier and move faster than usual. Anyway, Marie decided she was going to pee and she did. I was soaked and she was soaked from her pee and was all over both of us. I had put the bag with all her change of clothes in with the wheelchair which was who knows where on the plane. I had to sit in pee and Marie's nurse had put a diaper in a bag so at least I had that. I changed her diaper in my lap with the help of my mother-in-law and her nurse. I had to wrap Marie in a blanket to get her off the plane since the plane landed and we were in Florida. We got her into the wheelchair and found her bag with the change of clothes and found a restroom and changed Marie into dry clothes so she wouldn't be naked in the airport.

There was a man standing at the end of the hallway in the airport with Marie's name on it. We went up to him and he said he was a volunteer with Make-A-Wish and would show us to our luggage and van. We got to the van after carrying the fifteen bags and dropping half of them along the way. The van was a twelve-passenger van but Steve couldn't fit Marie's wheelchair in it. After throwing the wheelchair in, finally, he made it fit somehow, we all climbed in. The bags and people were all squished and we barely could all fit. We were stuffed like sardines in this van. We were finally off and going to where we were staying which was in Orlando.

When we arrived at the "Give Kids the World," it was unbelievable. The grounds were like we were in Candyland. They had little buildings with ice cream on them. They had a building that was a game room. There was a little train that went around the village. There was a little restaurant, and a carousel was next to a movie room. It was incredible. All the cute little buildings all adapted for children with special needs. Every building was handicapped accessible.

The little cottage we stayed in was a two bedroom with a pull-out couch and little kitchen. We went out for a walk and checked out the village, and Joe and Marie went on the train right away. Marie seemed to enjoy the ride.

We were going to dinner and I said, "Let's go in shifts." I hated to bring Marie to the Gingerbread House which it was called in the village to have dinner. I hated her not being able to eat so I stayed behind and Steve did too until the others came back to watch Marie. We went after everyone came back to eat our dinner. Marie was still tired and so we put her down to sleep around 8:00 p.m.

The next morning, Marie woke up and started looking odd; she looked so tired and she had a seizure. We thought she just was tired from the trip. Marie slept most of the day and we decided to just stay around the village so she could stay in bed and sleep. We went to the pool and had lunch and she was still sleeping when Steve, Joe and I came back. Her nurse then went to have lunch and Marie woke up but still didn't seem right. Marie was in "lock up" and just was droopy and stared out to nowhere. We took her for a walk to see if she would do better with the fresh air, and it was chilly, around sixty degrees and the weatherman said it was going to be in the forties that night. We were told Florida was seeing weather that was unusual for the state.

Marie didn't do well on the walk either; she was the same, droopy and staring. She was in what we call "lock up." Her hands were sweaty and her heart rate was up. Her nurse told us when she checked. We put Marie down for the night again, hoping she would feel better in the morning. Marie had two seizures during the night and woke up the same the next morning. She was in lock up, seizures sometimes meant she was getting sick or feeling sick. It was our gauge of her to notify us when she wasn't feeling well. Marie always had seizures when her system was down. I decided to call her doctor at home and see if he could give Marie an antibiotic, thinking she had a sinus infection. We never knew when she had a sinus infection because she didn't get fevers with them or have nasal drip with them either. Marie was just miserable and I felt terrible for her, especially being on this trip which was for her to enjoy. When I called the doctor, he said he would put her on an antibiotic as this has been the case before when Marie was not feeling herself. I went and got the medication for Marie at the CVS in the town and came back immediately and her nurse gave her the antibiotic. It was still early afternoon and we were on our third day. We decided to give her the medicine and give Marie a day to see if she feels better. We wanted to wait for Marie to feel better to go to Disney World or any of the other tourist places. Marie stayed with her nurse and grandmother and grandfather at the cottage which was what we called the place we were staying in. Steve and I took Joe to an alligator park, so he wouldn't get so bored waiting for Marie to get better. We had fun and Joe enjoyed the alligator park.

When we returned to the village, Marie was awake but still did not look very well. We took her for a walk and she just seemed to drag. We went back to the cottage and Joe went for ice cream with his grandmother and grandfather. I rocked Marie to sleep and then put her down for the night. As I was putting her down, she started to have a seizure and went to sleep. Marie slept through the night but had another seizure. The next day which was now, Thursday, we decided to take Marie to Disney World to see if that may turn her around and forget her troubles. Don't get me wrong, we all wanted to go to Disney World, but we had to wait and see if Marie was okay to go.

We got to Disney World and a woman came up to me in the Disney Park and asked me if I was with Make-A-Wish Organization, to which I replied yes. She must have noticed Marie and we were told to wear these tags on us that stated we were with Make-A-Wish Organization. Anyway, she asked me if Marie would like her picture taken with Snow White. Of course, I said, "Yes, she would love that." This woman then told me what time to go in the castle and get a picture with Snow White. When the time came, we got a picture with Snow White and Snow White was so sweet to Marie. Snow White said Marie had reminded her of a friend of her daughter, and Marie was so pretty. We all got a family picture with Snow White and when we went outside, Mary Poppins was there and asked us if we would like a picture of her with Marie. We said yes and Marie was just dragging and so droopy; she could hardly hold her head up. After the picture, we went and watched the parade and got ice cream.

By this time, Marie was exhausted and I was told there was a respite center where we could take Marie to rest. Joe wanted to go on the rides so Steve took him on the rides and we took Marie to the respite center. When we arrived at the respite center, after checking in and we were greeted by such kind employees, they asked if we wanted bottled water and if we wanted a movie put in for Marie. The room was like a Victorian style living room and very warm and cozy. I changed Marie and then held her in my arms; she fell asleep for two and a half hours. The nurse and I just talked to the other people coming into the respite center. Marie woke up and she seemed better and more alert.

Steve and Joe came in to find us and we left to go to the ride "It's a Small World," thinking Marie would really enjoy this ride. We got to the ride and there were a hundred people at least waiting for the ride. I thought we will be here all day. The attendant told us to come around the other side where the handicapped people were to go. There was no one there and the attendants immediately put Marie and me in a boat for the ride. Marie was slowly slipping away and going back into lock up and just staring to the side. The ride was a colorful musical and had so much for Marie to see, but I'm not sure she could take in any of it because she was so out of it. I tried to get her to see all the different countries and the music but Marie was off in her own world. It made us all sad to see Marie not feeling well still and not enjoying any of the trips.

We got off the ride and went to take pictures with all the characters. Marie sat through every pose and tried her best to keep her head up but just couldn't. We decided it was time to leave and get Marie some rest; she just couldn't hang in there any longer. I bought a blanket for Marie in one of the gift shops because she was so cold and it was getting chilly out. Keeping everyone together was a challenge in itself all day and I think everyone was tired. We left Disney World and got back to the cottage and put Marie down for the night.

The next day, Marie wasn't well either and it broke your heart because you knew this was a once-in-a-lifetime event for her, and we wanted her to enjoy herself. The Mayor was coming in to tuck the kids in. The Mayor was a character of the village, a big rabbit. This was a treat for the kids and we had signed Marie and Joe to have the Mayor tuck them him. Well, the Mayor came in and he is this big grey bunny and he had a little maroon vest on. When the bunny, the Mayor, Tom was his name, came into Marie's room, she looked at him like she was saying what the heck is this in my room, I'm trying to sleep. The bunny said to her, "Hi Marie, how are you?" Marie just looked at him and rolled right over to go back to sleep. The bunny grabbed her blanket to wake her and Marie pulled it back and looked at him again as if she was going to say to him, "I'm sleeping, do you mind?" We all laughed at Marie's reactions and the bunny went into Joe and Joe giggled and giggled when he saw the Mayor, this big bunny, coming to him. The bunny said, "Hello, Joseph, how are you?" and Joe just giggled and laughed. The bunny then got into Joe's bed and snuggled with Joe. Joe was delighted and it made his whole day.

The bunny left and we thanked him for coming to say good night to the kids.

The next morning, Marie was the same, not well. She was in total lock up and not herself still. We decided we were going to take Joe to another amusement park and leave the nurse and Marie at the cottage. It wasn't fair to leave Marie behind and it wasn't fair to take her with us and drag her around all day either. So we all agreed this was best, although I felt horrible leaving Marie and going to have fun. Everyone told me that she wouldn't enjoy the trip to an amusement park, but I still felt bad for Marie and for leaving her. I did not want Joe to feel that he was the cause of my sadness and ruin the trip for him either.

We got to the park and walked all day and Joe went on some rides with Steve and saw a parade. Joe had a great day and was thrilled to see the *Star Wars* exhibit. We then decided to go back to see Marie.

I said I wanted to at least take Marie into the pool when we got back to the cottage. I wanted her to feel the warm pool water because she never gets to go in a pool. The water is too cold usually and this pool was eighty degrees and would be good for her.

When we got back, Marie was the same droopy and staring off to the side. I was going to take her into the pool anyway and see if she might enjoy at least the pool. I got her in her new bathing suit I had just bought her for the trip, and she looked so cute in it. I handed her to Steve in the pool and she didn't really have any kind of a reaction. Marie seems to like it maybe a little although the air was cold and it was a cloudy day and maybe seventy degrees out if that. Marie was chilled and her nurse took her back to the cottage. We changed Marie and took her for a walk. This was probably the last time she would go for a walk here. We were due to leave in the morning and go home; our week was up in Florida.

They had a Christmas party on Thursday. They had it each week at the village for all the children and we took Marie and Joe to the party. The kids were getting their faces painted and the girls were being made up as Cinderella. I tried to get Marie involved, but she just turned her head when asked if she wanted to get made up like a princess. I knew Marie had enough and was tired. We went back to the cottage and packed to leave in the morning.

The night went by fast and the morning came and we were sad to see the week end. In a way, I was happy to go home, I have to admit. Marie just was not enjoying herself and it made me sad to have to face it each day and see her the way she was feeling.

We went to the village chapel with Marie before we left. To have Marie at the chapel gave us a sense of Marie was there and God was watching her. I guess I'm not really sure why but we had to bring her there before we left. We could feel all the children who had been there before as Dee and I had said, and maybe they too asked God for their blessing and asked God to take care of their child and watch over them. I am not the most religious person, but I do have my moments when I feel my belief in God.

We then thanked everyone for the wonderful week and said our good-byes to the staff at the village. We did have fun and saw a lot and Joe enjoyed it and maybe Marie did gain something from it; I think she did. We arrived at the airport and Marie was back on my lap on the plane headed for home. Marie decided halfway through the trip home again and she was going to have a bowel movement. It was disastrous and we apologized to everyone around us for the smelly bowel movement Marie just had. We again cleaned her up and we landed in the airport. Everyone around us quickly evacuated the plane because I don't think they could handle the smell any longer.

Marie seemed to be happy on the way home and back to herself. We couldn't believe it she was like the way she always was—content, alert, and just as happy to be with us. I said to the nurse and Steve, "Do you think she just had to have the bowel movement and her stomach was bothering her all week?" Steve said," It probably was just that and look at her, she's fine now." The nurse said, "I don't believe it, but it probably was just that, a little bit of out of her normal routine."

It was late by the time we got home, and everyone was tired. The airlines had called because they had lost Marie's car seat but called to say they found it on the plane and was headed back to Florida, but they would give us the car seat during the week.

All was well again and just another week, you would never know with Marie what the week will hold for her. She seems to be happy and glad to be back to her own bed and her routine the following days.

Just Another Day in Life

After coming back from Florida and trying to return to our normal lives again, Marie was back in school and doing her usual routine with the nurse. The next three months went by rather quickly with no real problems with Marie. We always had her seizures and ear infections but other than that, things were quiet for now with Marie.

It was May of 2008 and Marie was going to receive her First Holy Communion. I wanted her to have this sacrament because we are of the Catholic faith and I never knew what was going to happen with Marie. I had her baptized and I wanted her to have at least one more sacrament. The religious instructor who Joe had was so helpful in helping us fulfill our need for Marie to receive her first holy communion, and our parish priest was very understanding as well. Marie was not able, of course, to go to religious education nor was she cognizant of what First Communion is. I had found my First Holy Communion dress that I had worn. I wanted Marie to wear my dress and so after going back and forth to the dry cleaners to get the yellow out and fix a few pieces on my dress, it was ready for Marie to wear for her First Communion. I had found my wedding veil and had the dry cleaners make alterations for Marie to wear the veil for her First Communion. I had looked for dresses for her communion but they were either too formal or not enough. I just happened to come across my First Communion dress when my sister gave me a box of things my mother had kept before she died. I realized that I had to make my dress work and I wanted to have Marie in my dress but didn't know if I would be able to get the yellow out. Marie's aunt Debbie tried and Marie's grandmother tried and I did also and the cleaners and the dress finally was as white as it could be. The day came for Marie to receive her First Holy Communion and it was a great day. Marie seemed more alert and aware of what was going on that day in the church than she had in months. The mass was wonderful and Marie looked so beautiful in the white dress and my wedding veil trimmed to fit her little head. We had wheeled her up and the priest was so patient with her and so kind to Marie, he let her take her time. We were so proud of Marie and happy she could receive her First Communion.

I know Marie will not receive any more sacraments but I was so happy she could receive at least the two and she did. I want our children to also follow the Catholic faith. I know God is always with Marie and watching over her and so I want her to have the sacraments she is able to. You may wonder why I would have Marie go through this sacrament if she was not aware, but my faith tells me God is aware and she will go to heaven someday with her sacraments fulfilled as she could.

Marie was tired after her long day of receiving her First Communion and enjoyed the family coming to our house after to celebrate her day. We lay her down to rest and she slept soundly for a couple of hours tired from her busy day. Our family and friends went home and Marie was up again and I did give her a little of her cake which she really enjoyed and ate it very fast and did not choke. It was a long day for Marie, but she seemed to do so well. Everyone commented on how well Marie was today. Marie had to go to school the next day and she was tired, so we let her rest for the night to be ready to go in the morning.

The month went by and school was coming to a close and Marie had finished another year. Yeah! Joseph did also. The end of school always made Joseph happy. He was glad to be out of school for the summer like all kids are.

The end of June came and we had plans to have a vacation at a Connecticut shore. We had rented a cottage for the first time with Marie and hoping she would be all right. Marie never did well not being home but we thought we could try and see how it goes. We thought if Marie did not do well, we could always come home. It was only forty-five minutes away and the hospital was nearby that she had always gone to. Joe was really excited to be going to the beach for a week. Marie's nurse was staying nearby at a campground with her camper because she wanted to camp out and she would still be ten minutes away from Marie. We had also planned for Marie's nurse to come and take care of Marie during the day at the cottage.

It was June 28, 2008, when we rented the cottage. We were packed and ready to go. Marie was in her lock up state but we hoped she would do okay. I had to keep adjusting Marie in her car seat as she was as we call her "loopy." In other words, sagging in her seat and just spacey.

We arrived at the cottage and put Marie in the house so we could unpack; it was a hot day around eighty-five to ninety degrees. Marie never does well in the heat so we had asked if we could bring a small air conditioner to put in for Marie, the rental agency was not thrilled but said they would allow it for the week. So we get the air conditioner in and put Marie down for a nap to see if she feels better. We got settled in and Joe wanted to go swimming, and so Steve took Joe and went to the beach. I stayed with Marie and let her rest. It was such a nice quiet beach and had many activities planned for kids in the beach association. I knew it would be a great place for both Marie and Joe to enjoy for the week.

Steve and Joe came back and Marie seemed to feel a little more alert but still not totally herself. We had brought all her equipment and fit everything in the cottage for her that she would need for the week. Usually, it took two cars but we only had one as Steve could not use his company vehicle to go on non-business trips. It was a little difficult fitting everything in my van but we managed and had my father-in-law bring one piece of equipment in his van. The weekend went well and Marie did the best she could, although she did want to be held a lot and it seemed to comfort her. Steve was going back home because it was Sunday and he had to work all week.

We enjoyed the week and Marie's nurse came every day and took Marie for walks at the beach and she was okay, not great. We had a dilemma with Marie as there was no bathtub to bathe her in. The nurse and I had to put her in her wheelchair outside where they had a shower to bathe her. The bath was not her typical bath and Marie was uncomfortable with the bathing accommodations but she got through it like a champ. She always puts up with these types of situations better than we do. Other than that, we had a good time; the week was fun and Marie did fine. She wasn't terrible enough to go home and we had everything at the cottage that she had at home so we decided to stay for the week. My family and friends all came down to visit us and we had a great time. The week had come to a close and Joe and I were so sad to leave as we had such a great time all week. We actually did leave a night earlier because it was supposed to rain the next day and might be best to get Marie home in her own environment and she may perk up a little.

We were home and back to our routines. Marie waking up late and going for walks or outside on her swing, that she loved. Joe had swimming lessons and a reading program at the library and went to his grandparent's house to keep him busy for the summer.

The summer seemed to fly by and it was now mid-August and Joe was going to a resort in New York with his grandparents. Joe loved going away with his grandparents, aunt, and cousins for a week. He did this trip the last two years.

Marie would have all of our attention for the week which was nice for her, too. Joe never demanded a lot of attention anyway but it was just nice to have more time to give Marie. We snuggled with Marie and took her on walks and just had one schedule to keep the week Joe was gone.

I decided I wanted to surprise Joe and redo his bedroom while he was away. I had just finished painting our bedroom. I say "I" but I always drag Steve into my "little projects" as he calls them. Anyway, I decided to make Joe's bedroom a blue room which was more than I had thought when I started. I stayed up until one or two in the morning just to have the time to myself to finish the room. I had finally finished a day before Joe was to come home. I had recruited Steve at the end and made him work through the night to finish and get the bedroom finished and put all the furniture back in Joe's bedroom. I was exhausted and felt guilty not giving Marie as much attention as she needed toward the end of the week while I was busy painting. Joe came home from his trip and loved his new bedroom, and I was relieved to know that he liked his new room so much. Joe had a great time in New York and couldn't wait to show us all the pictures he had from his trip. His cousins made him a photo album for him of all the pictures they took on their vacation.

The weeks seem to come and go quickly and soon the school year will begin. Joe was not looking forward to school and I don't think Marie was either. Marie was getting used to the life of leisure in the summer. Marie woke up late and went to bed a little bit later and enjoyed relaxing and going out in her swing. Marie just liked lounging, I think; she seemed so content in the summer most of the time. Marie didn't do well with the real heat and we never let her go out in the hot sun. She is an air conditioner gal. She needs to be in the cool temperatures in the summer. She tends to have lock up and seizures when she is in the heat or exposed to too much hot weather.

School Begins with Difficulties and Relapse

It was August 29, 2008, the school year was supposed to begin for Marie and her brother Joe. Marie was now in the third grade, Joe in the second grade. Marie was ill with an ear infection and could not attend her first days of school. She was not off to a good start already. The ear infection did get better and the antibiotics were working as far as healing. Marie started having more seizures, too.

The following week, Marie was better and could begin school and her nurse was going to be with her all day.

Things were going pretty normal until one day I received a call at the school where I was working. I was now a substitute teacher for the town I live in. I was at work. It was three weeks into the school year and Marie's nurse called me and said that Marie was having many seizures. Her nurse told me she was having these weird seizures that only lasted seconds and stopped but had ten seizures in a matter of an hour. I told her to give her more Valium as she said she already gave her 10 mg of valium. The nurse watched Marie have more seizures after she phoned me but thought the Valium was now starting to work and stopping the seizures. I was worried so as soon as I got a chance to call an hour later Marie's nurse said that the Valium finally kicked in and Marie stopped seizing. Marie fell asleep and slept soundly for the rest of the day and all night.

The following day, Marie was tired but there were no seizures today. Marie had to stay home from school because she was so sleepy she couldn't keep her head up. As the day went on, Marie slept and by the end of the day, she woke up and looked more like herself and was alert.

Marie went to school the next three weeks and everyone was happy that she was back in school again. Marie's teacher tells me the children in Marie's class would miss her when she can't attend school and ask for her when she is out.

Things were going well and it was Friday morning, and I was due to go substitute a class and Marie's Friday morning sitter came, her name is Kathy. As I was about to leave, I decided to let my dogs out in the backyard so they could go out for a minute before I left for work. The day before, we had received about five or six phone calls from our neighbors telling us our dogs were out and running all over the street. Somehow, the little dog showed my big dog how to get out of the fence by climbing under it. So I figured after we fixed the hole the night before it would be okay to let them out. There also had been a raccoon up in a tree the day before and my dogs were trying to get it, but I didn't see it anywhere. I was in the house and the neighbors started to call and the police department telling me my dogs were loose. I ran out with my hair wet since I was still getting ready for work and then I start calling the dogs. Kathy is outside now calling the dogs in the front yard and no dogs. One of my dogs, Sam, is extremely large—about the size of a Great Dane—although he is a mutt a mix of German shepherd, lab, pit bull and every other breed I guess and weighs about 140 pounds. The other dog, Mally, is a golden retriever and as dumb as they come. So after not seeing the dogs and listening to my answering machine to find where the neighbors are calling from, I then jump into my van to go search the neighborhood. I am looking in the backyards of houses and asking neighbors if they saw the dogs and some gave me all different directions. A cop pulls up behind me and as I'm coming out of the back of a house and my hair wet and in a huge jacket of Steve's and ripped pants and looking like I'm robbing houses sneaking around to catch the dogs. The cop then says to me, "Can I help you, ma'am?" I then said to the cop, "I'm looking for my dogs." He then asked, "Are you Mrs. Fargo?" I, of course, said, "Yes, I am." He said, "We are getting calls that the dogs are missing and I'll help you find them." I then told him what they look like and I got in my van and kept driving around and stopping home to see if the now stupid, rotten dogs were home yet because I was going to kill them when I got them. Kathy is out in front telling me the police are on the phone and my father-in-law was just here and he is in his car looking. My neighbors called my father-in-law to get him in on the search now too, for what reason I'm not sure to this day. I got back in my car and still searching and now due to be at work in five minutes and still no dogs. The cop sees me driving around again and he does not see the dogs either. In the meantime, a neighbor calls and tells Kathy she thinks one of my dogs got a hold of the raccoon and the dogs are in her backyard behind our house. I then had to call the school where I worked to tell them I will be a few minutes late and I will be there. I run over for one last time to my neighbors in the back of my house and the husband is out front telling me the dogs were back there. I saw the two and as I yelled at them to come to me, they came running. I wasn't sure if I was going to hug them or scream at them. I was so relieved to have found them, so I could now go to work and hopefully not lose my job. One of my dogs looked a little banged up and looked like he and the raccoon had a wrestling match but the dog was okay, and I wasn't sure what ever happened with the raccoon. I think the neighbors called the humane society and they came and got it. I knew both my dogs had their rabies shots and were fine. Mally, the golden retriever, I knew was the culprit in getting this whole fiasco started. The cop came back to my house and I told him I had the dogs. I then found my father-in-law George and told him I have the dogs with me. I told Kathy, "Don't let them out no matter what." I ran out to work and was only a half hour late and thank goodness they understood when I told them what happened. Most of the time, people we know think when something is wrong; it is because of some problem with Marie. I told my work not this time. It was just another eventful morning. Kathy was a nervous wreck by the time I had left and grateful for me to having gone to work and not leaving her with the problem as I sometimes do.

Marie had been doing okay and going to school and feeling well until we noticed she was a little quieter than her usual self. We couldn't pinpoint what was the matter but knew something was different with her.

It was now the last week of September. On Tuesday morning, Marie woke up having seizures the same as before and I had witnessed what her nurse meant when she described these seizures. The seizures Marie was having came back to back every ten minutes and lasted seconds. When we thought she was done seizing and about to go to sleep, she would close her eyes and start seizing again. I watched these seizures go on for about two and half hours and the nurse was administering the Valium as fast as she could in between seizures. After giving Marie the 10 mg of Valium, we knew we could not do anything any longer to help Marie with stopping the seizures. It had been a long time since we had to take Marie to the hospital for seizures so I was thinking we could control these ourselves. I told the nurse I better call Marie's neurologist to find out what do we do next. I did not want to make Marie go to the hospital and get pumped with seizure drugs but knew I was running out of options. I had to leave a message in the doctor's office because none of the nurses picked up. I went back to Marie and the nurse. We were standing over her in her bed; she finally took a big breath as she sometimes does when she is done with her seizures. I turned to the nurse and said, "Do you think she is done? She looks more aware and is now responding to us." Her nurse said, "Yes, she looks a lot better and I haven't seen another one coming." A half hour passed and Marie had not had another seizure and was falling asleep. The nurse and I, it seemed, were both holding our breath for the last two and half hours while waiting for Marie to stop seizing. The phone rang and I looked on the caller ID, it was the doctor's office and the nurse said, "Is Marie still having the seizures?" I had told her, "No, she is done. I think she hasn't had a seizure in about thirty minutes now." The nurse then who knew Marie at the doctor's office had said she was glad Marie stopped seizing and if she starts again I should call an ambulance and bring her to the emergency room. I knew Marie wouldn't start again as that was not her usual pattern. Once she stopped, she usually didn't start right up again although we never know with Marie what she was going to do. These were a totally different type of seizures than Marie had before. Finally, forty-five minutes to an hour passed, we were still standing over Marie's bed and she was sound asleep. The Valium finally was beginning to take effect and calm the seizures down. I have been told by doctors. A seizure is like an electric explosion going off in the brain. The circuits and wiring in the brain are sending these signals to cause seizures in the brain. My definition is probably confusing but it is difficult to explain and since my daughter has so many varieties of seizures it is even more difficult to know what seizures are. We pretty much knew when she has rhythmic movements and has a certain look about her and you can't get her to focus. The doctors thought her lock up was a form of seizure too, but when she was in lock up, the doctor had an EEG test performed to see if she was having seizures. The EEG proved negative for seizures, so we know now she is not seizing during this time when she is in lock up as we call it. The doctor said he doesn't know what it is that Marie is doing when she is in lock up. The doctor watched and had me give her Valium during the EEG test to see if she came out of lock up and she did. The doctor saw Marie come to and said, "I don't know what this Marie is doing. I have never seen anything like this." We continued to give her Valium but had to stop when she was in lock up because she became so used to the valium that the Valium no longer could be used for seizures.

We used to give her the Valium for lock up once a week and about a year ago, we stopped. The Valium did start working again for seizures and she was no longer building up immunity to the Valium once we stopped giving it so often. The only reason I am explaining all this in case you wonder how we know the difference between lock up and seizures.

So back to Marie's day of the seizures, the activity did stop and Marie was awake in three hours and back to herself. We were used to this pattern as the next day, she slept off the Valium and seizures more than the first day. I think it is just the activity in her brain is so exhausting between the seizures and the Valium makes her so tired. She does sleep the first day or so if she doesn't wake up totally and she isn't great, she is groggy and will rest. The next day, she is always in a deep long lasting sleep for ten to fifteen hours at a time.

Marie, after sleeping for a day was okay and ready to go to school the next day. Marie went back to her routine at school and home for the next couple of weeks.

The next month went by and Marie started having the same seizures again lasting hours and the Valium not working. The nurse and I had counted thirty-five seizures before the Valium was taken. These patterns of seizures seemed to come for the next two months. We were due to see the doctor and explained it to him and he said to go up on one of her medications to see if that would help with the seizures which were occurring. The doctor had said this was probably a phase Marie was going through and the seizures would finally subside. I asked him also about her abilities, as we had noticed she was losing ground with any of the abilities she did have. I noticed that Marie no longer knew how to hold her bottle or cup; she no longer knew how to walk in her walker or wouldn't walk. The doctor had told me Marie will probably never get these abilities back and the seizures had probably caused the damage to make her no longer able to do what she did before.

The staff at the school Marie attended; who work with Marie had been fighting so hard and working with

Marie to keep up with all her daily activities. They also realized she can't do what she used to and told me this in a constructive way. The school staff had also been reporting to me about Marie's back as her spine is severely curved. I told them I am well aware of it and Marie did see an orthopedic specialist and is watching the curvature of her spine. I'm not sure if Marie's back is the cause of her not walking or standing in her stander.

Her doctor thinks it could be. I then informed the school that Marie will need surgery on her spine and the doctor is just waiting for her to grow more. So there is a lot going on now with Marie and we are watching everything and have all her doctors fully aware of each of her abnormalities because they are becoming more debilitating for her as she gets older.

The next few months go by and it is now February, and Marie is still having these terrible seizures. We informed the doctor and he put her on a new drug that has just been approved by the FDA. Marie as I said before can't go on new medications because she has been on all of the seizure medications there is in the United States. The new drug Banzel seems to be working and Marie hasn't had a seizure since being on it. Marie was doing well and was able to go to school more often now that she wasn't having seizures. Things were well again, we thought.

Marie was just about into the month of March and we noticed the seizures starting again. We gave her the Valium and it didn't work at all and after about three hours, she stopped seizing again. Marie slept a lot though the first month of putting her on the new drug. It must have calmed things down in her brain. Now the medicine was starting to reach its peak. It is wearing off again and the seizures are starting again.

It was Friday night and Joe was not feeling well with a cold. Marie started her seizures like I said and we figured maybe she was sick also; Joe could have given her his cold. Marie showed no signs of a cold or fever. We had nursed Joe all weekend and he was not getting any better. Joe started to bounce back on Monday and seemed better although he spiked a fever during the night.

I told Steve I was going to take both kids to the doctor tomorrow if Joe isn't better and Marie just doesn't seem right. Marie was sleeping all the time over the weekend and just too tired. I told Steve if I had to work, he and the nurse would have to take the kids to the doctor. I somehow forgot to mention on January 8, 2009, my husband had lost his job and was laid off. So Steve took care of the kids more and I was done with my master's degree and looking for a job. I was substitute teaching in the meantime to make ends meet. So anyway I did not get a call to substitute this day and took the kids to the doctor with Steve.

The doctor checked everything on Joe and said he had a cold and would be okay in a couple of days. Joe had a tendency to get bronchitis and pneumonia, so I just wanted to be sure he was all right. Then the doctor checked Marie and found she had an ear infection. I was amazed but glad the doctor had found something wrong with her that would answer why Marie was so lethargic. Steve was shocked too at the doctor's findings but was more shocked when the doctor had told us Marie would now need tubes put in her ears. The doctor said, "It is time for tubes in Marie's ear since she is having so many ear infections." The doctor checked Marie's chart (which is very thick and full from so many notes) and noticed that Marie was having ear infections almost every month to six weeks. When Marie's nurse and I had asked months prior if Marie needed tubes put in her ears for the infections, the doctor always said, "No, not yet." The doctor who just checked Marie gave us a name of an Ear, Nose and Throat doctor for us to take Marie to get the ear tube surgery. We left the doctor's office with the prescription and doctor's referral in our hand with Marie and Joe.

We were on our way home and Joe was bugging me to take him to the toy store and telling me how much better he was and that we could go and get a toy he wanted. I had to take Steve and Marie home and get Marie's antibiotic. We put Marie down because she was so tired. We did not know Marie had an ear infection as she never shows signs besides whimpering and she didn't whimper to let us know about this ear infection. Marie doesn't get a fever with her ear infections either so that's not a sign either for an ear infection. It is often hard to tell with Marie if she is sick because she can't tell us and we have to guess most of the time although we have become very perceptive and can tune in to when there is something wrong with her.

We know now we are facing two surgeries for Marie within the next two months. The surgeries she will have to undergo are the ear tubes and to get the plates out of her hip. We are hoping that we can get the two surgeries performed at the same time so Marie doesn't have to go through anesthesia and surgery twice. I'm not sure the doctors will do the surgeries together. I do remember Marie's orthopedic doctor telling us that she could take the plate out of her hip and have the spine surgery done at the same time if needed. So I am just hoping the doctors will do the ears and hip at the same time.

We knew there would be more surgery for Marie in the future as the problems seem to keep arising. I was just not planning on the surgeries coming so fast in her life. It seems just as Marie gets through one illness, she comes up with something else. We are now waiting for the appointments until each doctor decides on when the surgeries will occur for Marie. Either we do them together or separately; Marie will get through it as she always does.

Marie is still at home recovering from her ear infection. She sleeps most of the day and allows me to hold her and she takes a few sips of juice as she gets through each day with her ear infection. Marie started again around 11:00 p.m., the same day we took her to the doctor and found an ear infection, having the seizures all night during her ear infection illness, and I had to start giving her Valium. I held her hand and tried to get her attention but she was in this seizure state. I had to wake up Steve since Marie was not coming out of this seizure. I woke Steve and he came down to Marie's room and looked at her and said, "Yep, she is seizing and I don't know what we are going to do next besides take her by ambulance to the hospital to stop the seizures." I had told Steve how I just gave Marie Motrin on top of the Valium to see if that would help. I, finally, at 1:30 a.m., told Steve I'm going to lie down, wake me up in a half an hour if she doesn't stop seizing. Steve stayed with Marie and he said about 2:30 a.m., she stopped seizing. I had to go to work in the morning and just needed a couple hours of sleep, I thought. My phone was ringing at six in the morning as I slept through. The school I was supposed to go to wanted me in earlier, but by the time I got the message they had found someone else. I had apologized and told them I just shut my phone off upstairs when I know I am already working at a school. The woman who calls for subs was very kind and always understood when I had a problem with Marie. So anyway I went to work and called to check on Marie and her nurse said she was all right and sleeping. The rest of the week went on and Marie slept and woke for a little while each day getting better.

It was now Sunday, April 5, 2009, and we were due to go to two places at the same time. What I mean is Marie is supposed to go to an event at "Build a Bear" which was sponsored by a group called "Starlight Children's Foundation." Joe was to go to an Easter egg hunt with our church and then have his religion class. I woke up at 8:00 a.m. and heard Marie yelling out in her bed. I went down and she was cold but not wet. Usually, she will wake up to be changed when she is wet. I wrapped her up and she fell right back to sleep. I figured I'll let her sleep for an hour and then get her up for a bath and we will all go to the "Build a Bear" event. Joe said he rather go to "Build a Bear" instead of the Easter egg hunt and religion class. We discussed the choices the night before and I told him we couldn't do both. So I tried to wake Marie up at 10:00 a.m., and she was not moving. She was not getting up. I then went in and fed her through her tube and gave her medication. I thought that may rattle her but nothing, she wouldn't move. I kissed her and told her, "Time to wake up, Marie. Don't you want to go to get a bear?" Nothing. Marie wouldn't even move, she was snoring away. I told Steve, "Well, now what do we do? We can't even get her to one event for her to enjoy." The organization had other events in theaters but Marie would never understand or have the ability to sit through a show. We thought this "Build a Bear" would be fun for her to go as she has never been there. It was also nice that the event was for all kids who were disabled physically or mentally and Marie could not be an outcast. Well, I had to break the news to Joe and he was not pleased but said he would go to the Easter egg hunt and then religion class.

Joe had fun and enjoyed the Easter egg hunt, although when we came home and his father asked how the Easter egg hunt was? Joe said, "It was fun." I told his father how he gave up some of his Easter eggs to another boy who didn't have any. Joe's response was, "Well, you made me, Mom." I thought, *Great, Joe. I'm glad you're learning the spirit of giving.* Joe really is a giving kid. He was also mad at me because I had just had a discussion with him about not paying attention in religion class. So Joe was not happy with me when we came home. Poor Marie was still sleeping and it was now 6:30 p.m. We have been checking Marie all day and not sure what was the matter with Marie. She has not urinated since yesterday afternoon and she was on antibiotics. I'm now suspecting something was up again, possibly a urinary tract infection because she was on antibiotics. I will have to figure this one out; it will probably be another long night. The next couple of days went the same with Marie just sleeping and whimpering a little. Steve was going to take her to the dentist because she had an appointment the following morning. I told Steve if Marie is not doing well overnight she will have to go to her pediatrician to see if she has another ear infection. She never went back to sleep until 12:30 a.m. Monday morning so I knew something was wrong again as she was so fussy and couldn't sleep and yelled out once in a while. I gave her Motrin and it seemed to help her. She was able to sleep through the night. In the morning, I had to go to work but I had to call the pediatrician to see if one of the doctors could see Marie and check to see if there was something wrong again. The receptionist gave me an appointment for 1:00 p.m. I knew to make the appointment later in the afternoon as Marie had to go to her dentist at 11:00 a.m. I told Steve he would have to run Marie to the children's hospital at eleven and then run Marie to her pediatrician at one. Steve was not happy as I could understand it is quite the task to get Marie in and out of places and not so easy to get her in and out of the car and into her wheelchair. Steve did it though with the help of Marie's nurse. When they arrived at the dentist and the dentist was checking Marie's teeth, the dentist had found out that Marie's molars were coming in and she had three loose teeth. Steve told the dentist how Marie had been so fussy and the dentist had told Steve that the molars and the loose teeth were what were probably giving her pain. The dentist cleaned her teeth and told Steve to give Marie Tylenol for the pain. Steve then left the hospital with Marie and her nurse and quickly ran to the pediatrician since it was now twelve thirty, and Marie's appointment with the pediatrician was at one. Running into the doctor's office, the three of them—Marie, the nurse, and Steve—were rushing to make the appointment. The doctor saw them right away and examined Marie immediately. The doctor checked over every part of Marie's body and then looked in her ears and then found Marie still had in the ear that was infected, still with fluid that was residual from the ear infection. The doctor said the fluid may be making Marie uncomfortable and may need to be put on an antibiotic. The doctor told Steve he could wait and see how Marie does or put her on the antibiotic immediately, depending on what Steve wanted to do. Steve told the doctor he preferred to wait and see how Marie does and see if her teeth pain subsides also. They left the doctor's office and told the doctor they would call if Marie's condition worsens. Poor Marie between her ears and teeth no wonder why she couldn't sleep at night and was so fussy. When Steve had picked me up from work and told me about what each doctor said, all as I could think of was, you never know with Marie and it is so hard to figure her out at times. My Marie radar usually is better than that and I wish I had taken her to the doctors earlier but you never know with Marie. I always try not to run to the doctor for the smallest illness of Marie's and although lately I am kicking myself for not reacting when I know something is wrong with her.

Marie is still trying to overcome her ailments and seems to feel better with Tylenol or Motrin to help with the pain. Time will help heal her teeth so she will just have to grin and bear it until the teeth come in. Marie has a way of fooling us time and time again, and she will get through this as she does with everything else she bears. Our heart breaks and we worry all the time when she doesn't feel well. We have to wait and hope each day she gets better and she somehow does.

Marie will be ten on May 21, 2009, which is in a month; it is hard for us to believe. Marie has fought this lifelong battle for almost ten years now. I know she will continue to fight to the best of her ability as she does each crisis she comes across in her little life. I end this story of Marie's life and know with our help, she will continue to live to the best she knows how to. We don't know what will be in store for her, but know she will get through whatever life throws her way as she does remarkably each and every day. We do everything in our lives all for the love of Marie.

Epilogue

I have written this book to educate and allow people to experience our lives and the life of our child. There have been so many situations as I have described in this book which were so difficult to relive and express how much our Marie has had to endure. I wanted to let you know how much pain our family has had to live through. I also wanted to give some real examples of the ignorance of people in our society as far as dealing with a child with severe disabilities. Marie is such an unusual child and yet as normal as any other child. What I mean is that I wish at times she could have been treated as any other child and given the same considerations. It breaks my heart when I am given the look of people or say Marie is handicapped that is what we should expect in her life.

I have learned so much from Marie as I know my family and friends have. I too look at children who have special needs in a whole different light when I see them in a store or on the street. There is a human being in that body who feels and cries as we do just in a different way. I know that it took me a while to get to where I now understand children who I say are special. People always say God gave Marie to us for a special reason. I'm not so sure why she was given to us, but she has made our lives so much fuller and I will always be grateful to her for opening up my eyes to the world.

I have been bitter in my feelings toward others and had to experience many battles along the way to fight for Marie. I wouldn't have it any other way, I will continue to fight for her and to the best of my ability with every ounce of me, I will give her all I can. I have learned to ignore the people who are prejudiced against Marie and me and who label us. I may not like the prejudices or opinions that are held and thought but have learned to live with them. Even now as I write this book, I have a person who is not giving me an assignment to work as she doesn't think I can work, having a daughter like Marie, and still work in a competent manner. I have always left my problems with Marie at home and never carry them with me to work. At times, I try to educate people along the way as I see how ignorant and sometimes just downright stupid as far as dealing with children normal or not. I have learned to forgive and forget when people show unkind words or gestures toward Marie.

By writing this book, I would like to bring awareness and attention to the needs of children of multiple disabilities to the medical professionals and other professionals who work with these special children. What I mean in this statement is; I don't believe that the information the parents give about the disabled child is fully taken into consideration. The medical staff at times only hears what they believe is the problem and not what the parents of the child are trying to tell them. There have been many times as you have read in my book that I have had to constantly try to persuade the medical professionals to listen to me as I give them my daughter's symptoms and we are overlooked. I feel many times, Marie's suffering could have been avoided had the medical professionals listened to me and my husband. Many times, I have found that we know Marie and when she exhibits unusual behaviors and describe them to medical professionals we are not being fully heard. I have had to be so persistent when I know there is something very wrong with my daughter and have to battle the medical professionals or staff working with Marie. I know I don't have a medical degree and the medical professionals do but the parents of the child know their child and when something is not right with them. I have talked to many parents of children with special needs and have found the same problem with other parents or care takers that the medical professionals don't always listen to their concerns and have to fight to get the attention that their child needs. I am not saying that all medical professionals and staff ignore these problems. I have come across some incredible medical staff that have been so competent and understanding and treat us with the utmost respect and give so much attention to my daughter. Marie has some of the best doctors I could ever ask for. By no means do I want to discredit the medical professionals as they have saved my daughter's life many times. I just wish that there was more consideration given to the parents and caregivers by the medical professionals and people who deal with kids of special needs.

Above all, I have seen how kind and caring people can be toward my Marie. She is loved by so many and has been shown the utmost care given by people that amazes me also. The elementary school Marie goes to has had teachers and therapist who work with Marie who never quit trying. Marie's special education teacher, for example, tries to do the very best and will never give up on her and is always thinking of new ways to get Marie to develop and keeps trying to figure out ways to get Marie to learn. There are many therapists at her school who have worked so hard and one adores Marie and has come to the hospital and stayed for hours to make sure Marie was going to be all right. I can't say enough about the entire therapist staff and Marie's tutor about how wonderful they care for Marie and how they amaze me at their unwillingness to let Marie give up.

I also have to thank Marie's nurse at home who takes extraordinary care of Marie. Marie's nurse never misses a beat as far as knowing what Marie's condition is on each day. Her nurse makes sure she has every need met and will not settle for less. Her nurse grills the doctors until she gets the information she needs to make sure Marie is getting 100 percent care. We are so grateful to her for her caring ways and competent ability she gives to Marie every day.

I thank Marie's home physical therapist who works so diligently to give Marie the best physical therapy each week. Marie's physical therapist never gives up on Marie and strives to make Marie as mobile as possible. The physical therapist knows Marie very well and knows when Marie doesn't want to be stretched or move a muscle. The physical therapist always gets Marie to stretch or sit up most of the time. We appreciate the great work and care she gives Marie.

I thank Marie's case worker who always guides us to get Marie the benefits she is qualified to receive. Marie's caseworker is so kind and compassionate and is always there to help in any way she can.

Our family has been incredible and loves Marie unconditionally. They have all cried when Marie was down and laughed when she does something great. Her maternal grandmother, who I named Marie after, loved her and did everything she could to support me and Marie when things went wrong. Marie's maternal grandfather (my father) told me God gave Marie to me as a gift and to love her and care for her with all my heart. My father was right and he loved Marie and enjoyed her from the day she was born until the day he died. Marie's paternal grandmother and grandfather, I still look to them for guidance as they continue to love and care for Marie and deeply feels her pain when she is ill. They are always there for Marie and I will always be grateful for their love and kindness for Marie. I am also grateful for Marie's godparents, aunts and uncles, cousins and friends who are always there for her.

There is as much love as there is unkindness and I have learned to balance the two. I hope I am not too negative in regard to showing my feelings, and I know I have hurt some people's feelings in writing this book. My only intention was to educate and make one realize what pain they are inflicting when they don't understand and what may be going on is not what appears on the outside.